HIGH-
SPEED
SHUDDER

AN ANTHOLOGY

BRENT MONAHAN

HIGH-SPEED SHUDDER

Copyright © 2019 by Brent Monahan

Words Take Flight Books printing: 2019

ISBN 13: 978-0-578-60111-3

Printed in the United States of America

Fireflies first published in *Horrorzine* (1993)
Doctor, Lawyer, Kansas City Chief first published in *Robert Bloch's Psychos* (1994)
Shedding Light in the Black Forest first published in *100 Wicked Witch Tales*
The Shadow Knows first published in *Monsters From Memphis* (Zapizdat Press)
Sleigh Bells Ring first published as *In a Winter Wonderland* in *Horrorzine*
The Midnight Show at the Pink Palace first published in *More Monsters From Memphis* (Zapizdat Press)
The Fall of the Romanian Vampire first published by WTF Books

ALSO BY BRENT MONAHAN

DeathBite (with Michael Maryk)
Satan's Serenade
The Uprising
The Bell Witch/An American Haunting
To Move the World
Nevermore
Time Step
Love, My Neighbor
Illusions

The Novels of the Vampiric
The Book of Common Dread
The Blood of the Covenant

The John Le Brun Series
The Jekyl Island Club
The Sceptred Isle Club
The Manhattan Island Clubs
The St. Simons Island Club
The St. Lucia Island Club

PHOTO GALLERY

.

Fireflies

(From *Horrorzine*)

City folk. Suburbanites. They've killed too much of nature with their concrete sidewalks, asphalt streets and parking lots, decks and chlorinated swimming pools, their pesticides and herbicides. Remember all the birds of your youth, their colors and melodies? Remember how, on a hot night, you timed the chirp of the nearest cricket rubbing its hind legs together to attract a mate in order to estimate the temperature? Can you even hear them now? What about the butterflies? Not only the rare ones. The Common Buckeye, the Orange Sulphur, the Monarch, the Painted Lady, the Tiger Swallowtail? When was the last time you saw a Praying Mantis, you owners of McMansions?

So, what do these oblivious murderers do to "get back to nature"? They come out to the mountains and the rural lakes and the arts-and-crafts villages and ruin our lives during the best months of the year. You can detect their presence without even seeing them, by the amount of trash they throw out their car and camper home windows.

I own and run a country version of their convenience stores, a log-cabin-style 7-Eleven. I would love to serve only the locals, but there are – happily – not enough of us to make a living off of. So, I unwillingly stock the extras the Vandals, Visigoths and Huns neglect to pack: the toilet paper, condoms, beer and bottle openers. Also, the kitschy, down-home trash they haul home as souvenirs or gifts: the potpourri, "If Momma ain't happy/ain't nobody happy" class of kitchen hang-ups, the jump-a-peg games. But I refuse to sell three items that are too frequently asked for: butterfly nets, killing jars and ether. It isn't enough that they've exterminated all the flying insects in their own plastic world; they want to deplete our populations to the point of extinction for the fleeting fun of examination or just pure torture.

In other parts of our country there used to be a summer mania of catching lightning bugs, alternately known as fireflies, in Mason-type jars, until enough were crammed in to make a concentrated glow that one might even be able to read one's watch by. Now, of course, the time glows on the smart phone, and there's a flashlight built in, but reading the time is not the point; capturing wildlife and then leaving it trapped in the jar until it dies is apparently the goal. In the cities and suburbs they've killed off this source of merriment. But they resurrect their sport here with relish when they see the first winking in the twilight.

My store sits right between R29 and Lake Pindy. Exactly one square acre of property, which means my back wall is less than a hundred feet from the lakeshore. Ralph, the owner of the rent-a-boat enterprise next to me, is a good guy. He always backs me up when we see the butterfly nets and capture jars. We both say the identical thing: "Please don't catch the fireflies. We want Lake Pindy to be a place of life, not death."

And they look at us like we've been inbreeding for centuries and then glance down to see if we have six fingers. Some of them have even laughed in our faces.

"What's the harm, old man?" asked the leader of a recent pack – college kids, who looked like the gang from *Scooby Doo*. "They're just bugs. And they do reproduce, don't they?"

"Not when you trap them in jars and then forget to release them," I replied.

"Listen, fella," his buddy told me, "Where I come from, we used to pinch off the back ends that glowed and threw the front away, so it looked like a miniature collection of street warning lights."

"Don't tell me," I responded, "you've gotten civilized since then."

The little bastard did a slow sweep of my store with his judgmental eyes and said, "Certainly more civilized than you."

The leader touched his friend on the shoulder. "Bro, lighten up. When in Droolsville, do as the mouth breathers do." He smiled at me. "We'll try to remember to let them go after we're done…providing we're not too drunk."

They, naturally, lacked any bills or change and paid with a debit card. I watched with appreciation as their two female companions undulated toward the front door with the bottoms of their butt cheeks protruding from their short-short shorts.

I kept an eye on them through the front window, until I was sure the pack was sauntering toward Ralph's Boat Rentals. Then I picked up the phone.

"Ralph? It's me," I said. "You got four Einsteins headed your way. You ought to know they came in here asking for a Mason jar to catch lightning bugs." Ralph made an unhappy sound. "I gave them my usual lecture, but they're determined. Bought a jar of mayonnaise, which I'm sure they'll pour onto the ground, rinse out and then soak the label off."

"I could say everything's rented," Ralph said.

"That's up to you. Or you could rent 'em the General Slocum."

"I'll see how they treat me. Thanks," he said and rang off.

I took care of a couple of customers but glanced now and then at Ralph's place. Sure enough, Ralph had rented the four the most repainted, flat-bottomed aluminum boat in our state. Its engine was a low-horsepower trawler, the hitch of which Ralph had customized to stand an extra foot away from the stern. The two guys piled into the boat, half listening to Ralph's instructions on working the engine and observing proper water safety and courtesy. They managed to start the motor and steered off toward Sunset View Campground, which lay just around a promontory that hid the neon-lit eyesore from our sight. The two young women jumped into their late-model, flashy-red Mustang and scattered several buckets of gravel in leaving Ralph's parking lot.

I keep my place open until 10:00 p.m. during tourist season, letting my nephew open up at 7:00 a.m. and myself working from 1:00 p.m. until closing. My long hours are worsened by the guff I take from our invader lords and masters who think it's "fun" to leave their air-conditioned homes and offices, their Starbucks and Au Bon Pains, and their personal trainers at the gym to "rough it" for a week. But I do get to view the aforementioned sunsets in the distant pine trees on the opposite side of the lake, see the flights of egrets, geese and loons, and also enjoy the lake follies of the human loons from time to time.

Such was the case on this evening. From around the promontory came the General Slocum, with its four boisterous sailors doing their unlevel best to tip the boat over with their erratic, drunken movements. The pilot, who was the nastier of the two males, throttled the engine down, then shut it off and let it drift to where I had a perfect view. Clearly, they thought it would be oh-so-funny to show me just how little they thought of my advice about catching lightning bugs, or fireflies – which they thought were the same thing. I know this because the blonde, buxom beauty with the rounder butt held up the now-clear-walled mayonnaise jar for me to see. It was already three-quarters filled with the little creatures who had glowing rear ends. But that was not enough. They had managed to get their paws on not one but three of the sort of net wands used in pet shops to capture fish. To my amazement, in spite of the erratic darting of their quarry over the water and their obvious drunkenness, the quartet was going for a new record in flying bug jar density.

The hour was 8:00. Ralph usually closed at 7:00, but he had stuck around. I like to think that he has a sixth sense about the likelihood of such momentous occasions. He stood about twenty feet from the shoreline, staring at the display with his arms crossed, calm as could be.

"They're pretty close to shore," I said. "Don't you want to take a couple more steps back?"

"Nah," he replied. "That's a Hellman's medium jar, ain't it?"

"Yep."

"Here's more than far enough."

The leader, who held the jar, was particularly adept at clapping the lid down after each new bug was added. Few escaped. The jar pulsed brighter and brighter. The two young women oohed at the primitive entertainment.

"Wanna bet on how much longer?" I asked.

"Sure. Ten bucks says less than three minutes."

"You're on." I consulted my watch.

The seconds ticked by. I really did think I had it won this time. Two-minutes, fifty-two seconds passed, and I drew in a big breath to celebrate my shrewd calculation. Two seconds later, Ralph won.

All four of the urban wise guys were standing when it happened. First came the lightning, as critical density was reached. The jar exploded with a tremendous noise that echoed across the lake, sending glass and metal flying at lethal speeds in all directions. All four would-be bug killers hurtled backward into the lake. The screams from the pain of the penetrating shards and the instantaneous second-degree burns were punctuated by coughs as one after the other inhaled water from the waves they had caused. All of them had managed to stay conscious. They did what they could, splashing, paddling, even swimming toward the boat for their salvation. None had bothered to don the life vests Ralph had provided. The problem was that they had captured not just our county's singularly dangerous lightning bugs but also our own unique species of fireflies, as well. The inside of the boat, which Ralph periodically protected from rust with a petroleum-based coating, was completely ablaze.

Even in August, Lake Pindy is darned cold. After the sun goes down, the mountain air also gets chilly fast. These factors, combined with the grievous wounds from the glass and metal and the burns, ensured that the four bug-catchers did not make it to shore, even given that they were less than three hundred feet out.

"Yet again, Sheriff Art and the rest of the town council will make sure this news don't get across the county border," I recited.

"Would kill the tourist business and turn Lake Pindy into a ghost town," Ralph said, which was the chorus to my verse. "You warned 'em; I warned 'em," he said calmly, as if that were enough to exonerate us. "'Please don't catch the fireflies. We want Lake Pindy to be a place of life, not death.'"

"Maybe we should add one more word," I suggested. "Not 'your' death."

"Oh sure. That would scare the cocky know-it-alls. How many New Yorkers died with the real General Slocum fire?"

"One thousand and twenty-one," I reminded my friend.

"Let's see. These four bring our total up to thirty-six. A long way to go."

I handed Ralph the ten dollars I owed him and affected a hillbilly drawl, even though Lake Pindy is nowhere near the Southern Appalachians. "Cheer up, good buddy. Them flatlanders is gettin' more sadistic and uppity every year. I say we reach fifty by end of next summer…if your General Slocum holds up and you don't run out of aluminum paint."

Doctor, Lawyer, Kansas City Chief
(From *Robert Bloch's Psychos*)

Vince Martelli stood stock still in front of the oak door, leaning well out over his Gucci loafers with his right hand extended in mid-air, like a plastic figure on a model railroad layout. What had paralyzed him was not the name on the door's bronze plaque but the initials etched below the name: M.D. "Fritz Nussbaum/M.D." Medical doctor. The person you went to when you were sick. Except that Fritz Nussbaum was a psychiatrist. A doctor of the mind. Walking through the door signified an official admission to himself that Vince no longer had any doubts. Once he crossed the door's threshold, he acknowledged at least partial responsibility for the nightmare that had muscled its way into his waking existence.

Vince drew in a deep breath. "Hut one; hut two," he said, softly but with the same kind of diaphragmatic kicks he had used to be heard at the line of scrimmage over stadiums filled with roaring fans. He wrapped his bear-paw hand around the knob and rotated his wrist. The door was locked.

With a twist of his other wrist, Vince exposed his solid gold Rolex. Six after six. Damn! Could the doctor have left already? It had taken every ounce of nerve Vince possessed to call Nussbaum's receptionist this noon and make the appointment. She had said "Doctor" preferred seeing patients during the daytime, especially on a first visit, but there was no way he could afford to walk into such an office while other people were there. Not Vince Martelli. He had capitalized on both his professional vocal presence and the genuine panic he could hear in his voice to convince the receptionist that Dr. Nussbaum could indeed see him the same evening, at six o'clock.

So, where is the son of a bitch? Vince wondered, as he snatched a handkerchief from his coat jacket pocket and wiped away the beads of sweat that had accumulated on his forehead. Parking his 4x4, walking across the lot into the commercial building's lobby and taking the only elevator (mercifully meeting no one the whole way) had consumed four of the six minutes. Nussbaum would have to have left near the stroke of six to have avoided him.

Vince balled his huge hand into a fist and slammed it against the door. And then it occurred to him that maybe Nussbaum hadn't had a 5:00 p.m. appointment. Maybe he had taken a seventh inning stretch to catch a bite at a restaurant over on Route 1. Or to hoist a beer at a nearby bar. Sure as shit was where he'd be this time of day, at least if he was on the road. Growling, Vince pushed off the door and pivoted toward the elevator.

The door opened behind him.

"Mr. Smith?"

Vince spun around. Even though the man stood squarely in the center of the doorway there was loads of room, around him and above. He couldn't have stood more than five-foot-seven, which was half a foot shorter than Vince. A head of thick, teased hair might have given him some stature, but the guy was bald as the proverbial billiard ball. Bald, bespectacled, bow tied and bowlegged. Vince imagined Nussbaum stripped of the armor of this expensive three-piece suit, standing on some Jersey beach wearing only a pair of swim trunks. Bullies from neighboring states would be trucking to kick sand in his face. But aside from being bald, bow tied, bespectacled and bowlegged, he had a reputation for big brains – and that was all Vince required of him.

Vince braced himself for the inevitable look of recognition, but it didn't happen.

"Mr. Smith?' the man repeated.

"Yeah. That's me."

The man took a couple steps backward. "Come in."

As Vince walked into the waiting room, he noticed for the first time the security peephole in the door. Nussbaum had probably been watching him for the past minute, trying to figure out why a big-time celebrity was standing at his door instead of Jack Smith. And then he had figured it out, realized the need for a pseudonym. He was merely playing along. That had to be it. Weirdness in a psychiatrist's office was the last thing Vince needed right now. Vince relaxed enough to note that the receptionist's desk was empty. Just him and the shrink.

"Please, take a seat," Nussbaum bade, gesturing to one of the spindly, Bauhaus-type chairs to Vince's left. He closed the outer door behind him and crossed with a rolling gait to the receptionist's desk, off of which he plucked a clipboard and pen. He presented them to Vince.

"I'll need you to fill this out," Nussbaum said.

Before Vince could reply, the doctor was moving to the inner door. "I'm on the telephone with a patient," he explained. "Try to relax." His slender figure slipped through the doorway.

Try to relax. Yeah, sure. Easier said than done. He must have seen the sweat pouring off Vince's head. Vince set the clipboard on the desk and moved toward the large mirror on the wall behind the chairs. For sure. Plenty of perspiration. His focus lowered to the skin under his lake-blue eyes. Then to the angle of his well-chiseled chin. He thrust his jaw forward, forcing the skin taut, and held the unnatural position for several moments then let go, shooting himself a grim expression.

Nussbaum had not completely shut the inner door. For a few moments, Vince had been oblivious to the psychiatrist's half of the conversation drifting out. But it started to sound too interesting not to eavesdrop.

"Lorelei, we have been over this a hundred times."

Vince sidled toward the door.

"No, in fact, that does *not* count for anything. The situation is still fundamentally the same. You're in a destructive, dangerous relationship and you must leave him."

During the following silence, Vince returned to the clipboard and took it in hand, as if he actually intended to fill it out.

"Don't start that old game, Lorelei. I told you how. You have the telephone number, but if you need it again, I…Just by doing it. Lots of women have gone through this before you, and with fewer resources. You're more afraid of your inability to survive on your own than you are of him, but that's irrational."

Vince circled the desk and approached the half-dozen diplomas and certificates under glass that hung on the wall. Impressive as hell. Yale. U of Penn. Diplomate of this. Board member of that.

The woman must have interrupted again, but Nussbaum's patience was clearly wearing thin. "Listen to me…Listen! When does he return? All right, that gives you another day. Come in tomorrow at ten and we'll make the arrangements together. You can. Yes, you can. No more excuses. Tomorrow at ten. Good night."

Vince glanced again at his Rolex. Sounded like a battered wife. Probably close to what Cindy had told her shrink, even though he'd never laid a hand on her. Fists through walls, plenty of psychological warfare on both their parts – but never any marks on her. He was too smart for that. Not with all his hard-earned worldly possessions riding on the outcome. Never let himself get that out of control. Until now. Twelve damned minutes after. The clock had better not start until he got into that office. He heard the telephone receiver meeting its cradle. He thought about moving but realized he'd boxed himself in. There was no way of escaping the pocket.

Nussbaum came through the door and found Vince reading the diplomas.

"Expensive paper," the psychiatrist remarked. "If you have some intelligence, enough time and money, they give you those as prizes."

"You're being modest, Doc," Vince said.

"Not entirely," Nussbaum countered, moving to the clipboard. "I don't want you to think my discipline is like a dermatologist's. I can't prescribe you some tetracycline and promise your inner blemishes will clear up in a week."

"I'm not here for –"

"You haven't filled out these forms, Mr. Smith."

Vince cocked his head, unbelieving. "You are kidding me, aren't you?"

"What do you mean?"

"I mean we can both dispense with the deception." The doctor's face remained blank. "You do watch television, don't you?"

"Not very much. PBS. The Discovery Channel."

It wasn't the first time in his adult life that someone failed to recognize him, but Vince could count such incidents on one hand. If the guy had said he was a rabid football fan, the situation would have been mortifying – but he was, after all, just a shrink.

"I'm Vince Martelli."

Nussbaum's eyes semi-brightened. "You're the sportscaster!"

"Right. And I didn't fill out your sheet there for two reasons. First, I'm not gonna be a long-term patient; and second, I'm paying for this session with cash. I can't have it on my health insurance record."

Nussbaum stepped to the side of the door. "We can talk about that later. Come in, Mr. Martelli."

"Vince."

Vince strode into the office. It was large and contained its expected huge desk, decorated with a banker's lamp and matching mahogany frames, turned so he couldn't see the photos they held. In front of the desk was a pair of curved-backed chairs. A bookcase filled with heavy-duty textbooks and journals covered the wall to his left, and, to his right, three good Matisse reproductions under non-reflective glass hung above a leather divan.

"The classic couch," Vince exclaimed. "I thought it was such a cliché by now…" He let the remark trail off.

Nussbaum snatched several tissues from a box sitting on a wooden tea trolley near the door. "Perhaps you'd like to wipe your forehead?"

"Thanks," Vince said. "I'm more nervous than the time I faced Alabama for the SEC title. I was a Heisman Trophy candidate, y'know."

"No, I didn't." Nussbaum had reached for something else on the trolley. When he turned, Vince saw that it was a circular, brown plastic bottle. He was opening it and tapping out its contents.

"What's this?" Vince asked.

"A beta blocker. Mild chemistry, to help you relax and get more out of our talk."

"Mild? Then you'd better give me two. I'm big."

"That you are," Nussbaum said, offering two of the tiny, white pills. "I imagine you got used to pills if you played big-time football."

"Not as much as most," Vince answered, proudly. "I stayed as healthy as anybody in the

NFL. The only bad time I had was when a tackle broke my leg." His eyes continued to roam the room, past the desk to the wall of glass that looked down on the building's parking lot and the landscape-divided professional complexes of Metropark, New Jersey. His eyes widened at the sight of a brass telescope mounted on a wooden tripod. It was apparently not enough for this guy to get his jollies prying into people's minds; between sessions he spied on the activities in the lot and inside other offices.

Nussbaum had found a pony-sized bottle of Perrier on the cart and was twisting off the cap.

"Don't bother dirtying a glass," Vince offered. "I can drink from the bottle."

"How big are you, Vince?"

Vince swallowed the pills. "Six three. Two twenty six. Only gained twelve pounds since my pro days."

"Admirable. Would you prefer to sit or lie down?"

"I'll take the couch," Vince elected, handing the physician the empty bottle. He lowered himself onto the cool leather, completely covering its upper surface.

"What's bothering you, Vince?" Nussbaum asked, once he had crossed the line, defined by the back end of his desk, that separated his inviolate half of the office from that available to the patient.

Vince sucked in a substantial breath. "First, I want to be sure about something: psychiatrists are like priests and lawyers, right? I mean, whatever I tell you, you can't bring to the police...or they can't make you talk later on."

Nussbaum looked out the window. "That's correct. Whatever you have to say here is totally confidential. Please, try to relax."

"Okay. It started with a piece of mail I got at my apartment. It wasn't junk mail...y'know, addressed to 'Occupant.' This was expensive stationery. My name and address were handwritten. But it was still an ad. It called itself a confidential letter, from Dr. Milton Kronenberg. You know the name?"

"Should I?"

"No. I guess not. He's a plastic surgeon. Park Avenue. Very high priced, very exclusive. The letter talked about the importance of looks and youth, in society and the business world. It assured that 'body enhancement'...his phrase...had become commonplace, and nobody thought of it as vanity anymore."

"How did you feel when you read the letter?"

Vince rubbed his hand along the line of his jaw. "I was teed off. The nerve of this SOB. I mean, this wasn't some form letter sent out to every house in my zip code."

"How old are you, Vince?"

"Forty eight. But a pretty fantastic forty eight, don't you think?" When Nussbaum failed to respond, Vince persisted. "Right?"

"What I think doesn't matter," Nussbaum said, still staring out the window. "What's important is the depth of your reaction."

Vince's hand strayed to his forehead. At least he had stopped sweating. "Maybe I didn't make myself clear. I was pissed at this guy's nerve at contacting me unsolicited. I mean, that's still unethical in the medical profession, isn't it?"

"Public advertising is. A private solicitation is shady ground. Did you do anything about the letter?"

"I tore it into a hundred pieces and tossed it in the garbage."

Nussbaum swung around and headed toward his high-backed, tufted-leather chair. "But you continued to think about it?"

"No way. Life is too short to waste on petty annoyances. But then the bastard calls me!"

"Really?"

"Oh, yeah. Let me give you the conversation verbatim, okay?"

"Please."

"He goes: 'Vince Martelli?' I go: 'Who is this?' He goes: 'I'm surprised you haven't responded to my letter.' Instantly, I know who it is. And I'm doubly teed off, because I have an unlisted number. I go: 'How did you get this number?' He goes: 'I was given it by the same friend of yours who's concerned about your career. I had to agree with him, Mr. Martelli: The booze and the years are starting to show around your eyes and your chin.'" Vince lowered his shoulder and craned his neck around to appeal to the psychiatrist with his eyes as well as his voice. "Can you believe it?"

"And how did you reply?"

"I told him I was gonna report him to the AMA and that if the day ever came when I did want plastic surgery, he'd be the last one to know. Then I slammed down the phone."

"And...?"

"Five minutes later the asshole calls again. Calm as anything, he says, "I've done Don Meredith and Frank Gifford, y'know. I can keep my mouth shut if that's what's bothering you.' To that I replied that if he ever called my condo again, I'd personally and permanently shut his mouth for him.""

"You threatened his life."

Vince's jaw worked up and down. "Not really." The vehemence in his voice was gone, dissipated by the psychiatrist's question. "It was just the kind of thing that automatically comes out when you're attacked."

"Was it an attack?"

Vince sat up. "Shit. I knew I'd have to be careful what I said in front of you. You shrinks assume whoever walks through your door has the problem."

"I assure you, I'm assuming nothing. Go on, please."

"My answer was just a knee-jerk reaction, okay? Like guys shout at each other across the line of scrimmage. Punch/counterpunch."

"This comment of his about booze…do you drink heavily, Vince?"

Vince changed his focus from the psychiatrist to the bookcase. "Depends on what you mean by 'heavily'."

"More than a six pack a night. Or more than three double bourbons. I talk in terms of my size."

"Do you ever indulge in more than three double bourbons?"

The psychiatrist's monotone voice, coupled with an insistence on focusing everything back on

Vince, was beginning to truly irritate him. "What's your point?"

"I agree that you were being attacked when this caller mentioned liquor. The sharpness of the attack, however, hinges upon the actual level of your normal consumption."

Finally, the shrink had conceded him a point. Vince suddenly felt as if he needed to get more peaceful, to press his back into the couch. He reclined again.

"Right, right."

"I take it this was not your last incident with Dr. Kronenberg?"

"Absolutely. But first I've got to tell you about something else that happened to me, because I'm sure it's important."

"Go on."

"About a week after those phone calls, I was home…it's off-season for football, y'know. I live in a big golf course condo over in Short Hills. I'm watching ice hockey on the tube, drinking a second bourbon, and suddenly I'm asleep. One minute, it's the second period; the next, it's morning. I figured I was just bushed. But when I went down to the parking yard, my truck wasn't in my private space. I thought it had been stolen. Then I spotted it in the next lot over. Nothing was missing, but…"

"Who else has the keys to your truck?"

"No one. I drive a loaded Toyota Land Cruiser. That thing's my pride and joy. I'm sure you can see it out your window. Nobody but me ever drives it."

"I see."

Vince let in a long, slow breath. Despite having to relive the harrowing tale that had driven him to this couch, he was feeling calm. Really calm, for the first time in days. Bless "Better Living Through Chemistry".

"So, I immediately go out to the golf course to play a round and everything's fine. But that afternoon, when I walk into my kitchen, I find a bag on the counter from a pharmacy I never deal with. Inside the bag are three different tubes of those new wrinkle removing creams."

"How do you think they got there?"

Vince flung up his hands in frustration. "I must have gone out in my truck the night before and bought them. Like sleepwalking."

"Did you go to the pharmacy and ask if anyone recognized you from the night before?"

"Are you kidding? No." Vince curled up the corner of his mouth and shook his head slightly. As if Vince Martelli could afford to stroll into a pharmacy and ask if he'd been acting like an amnesiac. "What I did was cut back on the sauce. I knew Kronenberg was full of shit about my face, but it couldn't hurt to give my liver a rest."

"Sounds reasonable to me."

Vince grimaced. From here on, it was rough sailing. "But I started having this recurring dream about my skin. In the dream I'd go into my bathroom to shave. I'd shoot lather into my hand and put it to my chin. Then I'd look in the mirror and my skin was like an elephant's. Grey. Thick. Incredibly wrinkled."

"Dr. Kronenberg had gotten to you."

"Clearly. And still I pushed it all aside. Give it time to fade, I told myself. But then, about a week later, I was up with my lawyer and agent at Fox TV headquarters, to hammer out the next season's contract. You probably can't appreciate it, but these negotiations are a bear, no matter how many times you go through them."

"I would assume it actually gets more difficult every year," Nussbaum replied.

Maybe Nussbaum did appreciate the process, Vince reconsidered. The doctor knew his age and, therefore, knew approximately how long it had been since the name Martelli had been a thing of idolatry for football fans. His value as a sportscaster was rapidly reducing to his voice, his color commentary, and his looks alone.

"It's always difficult," Vince said, evenly. "What made this intolerable was one of Fox's slimy lawyers beginning the negotiations by smiling and saying, "What have you been doing in the off-season to piss off the fans, Vince?' Seeing he's got me off balance, he says Fox has gotten piles of letters commenting on my 'alky looks'."

"I refuse to open negotiations until this 'pile of letters' is rounded up. It turns out to be a total of three. One posted in Boston, one in New York City, one in Saddle River. They're all dated after Kronenberg's phone call. Each is on different paper. One's from an old ribbon typewriter; one from a laser printer; one handwritten, but as if the writer used his opposite hand. I demand photocopies of the three letters. They tell me I'm acting crazy and that's strictly against company policy. The negotiations are over for the day. It doesn't take much checking to learn that Kronenberg lives in Upper Saddle River. The zip code on the letter mailed from New York City is the same one as his office. Probably had a conference in Boston and mailed the third one from there."

"What do you do about this?"

"I march right up to his fancy office, push my way past his receptionist, and catch him at his desk reading Dow Jones quotes. He recognizes me right off, jumps up and sticks out his hand. I wasn't expecting that. It took a little wind out of my sails…enough so I didn't punch him out. Thank God. But I let him know I was on to his letter-writing campaign and if he did one more thing to me I was gonna sue him into the poor house." Vince listened to his voice as he spoke. It was incredibly calm, as if he were speaking of an incident whose emotionality had been dulled by a passage of decades. Those little pills had really kicked in.

"Let me guess," Nussbaum said, from his power position behind the desk. "He denied the whole thing."

"Hey…you're good, Doc! That's absolutely what he did. A cigar store Indian couldn't have played it more deadpan. When I told him I didn't appreciate the act, he said I should see a psychiatrist – that I'd been overcome by delusions."

"And you took his advice?"

Vince blinked several times. His eyelids were becoming heavy. "No, of course not. I figured he was using a classic offensive defense – but that was all right with me, as long as he knew I meant business. That was three days ago. I went straight home. Worked out in my private gym for an hour or so to blow off steam. Felt better. Put on the highlights tape of me QBing the Chiefs in the '74 season and knocked down a few bourbons. Next thing I know, it's morning again. Another fourteen hours unaccounted for. I go down to check on my truck. It's in my reserved space, but I swear it looks like it's been moved. Parked farther to the left than I normally steer it in. I check my apartment, top to bottom. Nothing seems out of place. My golf bag's already in the back of the truck, so I head out to the clubhouse. Join a twosome. Second hole, I need my five wood. Take off the cover. There's blood all over the head. My buddy, Walt, sees it first and asks me who I killed. The other guy, Teddy, is laughing so hard it gives me a second to recover. I say it must have been the maid. I tell them a rat's been working over the garbage out back, and she must have used the club to nail it. I wash the head off in a water hazard nearby and do my best to concentrate on the game. But I'm really spooked." Vince raked his splayed fingers through his thick hair. "When I get into the clubhouse, I call Dr. Kronenberg's office, give them a phony name and say I'm from the AMA and need to speak to him. The receptionist tells me he hasn't come in. Her voice is edgy. I keep probing until she admits he was supposed to be there, but no one – including his wife – knows where he is. Later, I checked my truck and found a couple more drops of blood. In the bottom of my golf bag, I found a handkerchief with Kronenberg's initials on them."

Vince tried to sit up, to be able to look at the psychiatrist when he delivered his next sentence, but the effort was too great. "I tried to remember and I can't. Nothing. The reason I'm here is to ask you about these blackouts. Can you do any kind of test to prove I get them?"

"I'm sorry to say there is no such test, Mr. Martelli. Perhaps, if you were to drink heavily in front of licensed physicians and they could monitor you...but you only blacked out twice, correct?"

"Yes."

"Then the blackouts probably had to do with your mental state and not the alcohol. I doubt seriously that they could be recreated."

"Shit. You understand that the police will be knocking on my door any minute now? I understand they don't do much the first twenty-four hours someone is missing, unless it looks like a crime's been committed. But then, even if they don't find him, they're gonna start asking questions. His receptionist recognized me. She musta heard me yelling...even if Kronenberg didn't talk about me afterward."

I understand. And you were completely alone during the second blackout?"

"Of course. Christ! If I'd had someone with me, I wouldn't be here."

"All right. Can you sit up?" Nussbaum asked, rising from his chair.

"I don't..." Vince made an effort. "Do I have to right now?"

"No. Mr. Martelli, at any time since your first blackout, did you check your house for signs of entry, for listening devices and the like?"

"No," Vince said, confused by the man's bizarre change of tack. "What do you mean?"

"I mean that both you and Dr. Kronenberg could have been set up. Someone wanted both of you punished and cleverly arranged to make it look like one killed the other."

Vince laughed at the absurdity of such comic relief being offered by a top-flight psychiatrist. "I thought I was the crazy one, Doc! Why would anyone do that?"

"Perhaps you both have some negative quality in common."

Vince raised his wrist lethargically to consult his Rolex. Plenty of time left in the hour. He could tell that this much-dreaded confession he had disgorged would have to be repeated…to another shrink or the police. Because Nussbaum's specialty was obviously paranoia. And fantasies. Might as well hear the guy out, since was paying for the full hour.

"What negative quality would that be?" Vince invited.

"Heavy drinking, of course. Dr. Kronenberg is also a heavy drinker."

At this news, Vince managed to heave his bulk over onto his right side, so that he could see Nussbaum's face. "I thought you said you didn't know him!"

"No. I asked you why I should know him. I was less than honest, I'll admit – but I didn't want that piece of news to muddy your story. I've come to know him quite intimately, in fact. He not only drinks, but he also firmly believes that he is in complete control of his drinking. As you do. Which makes you both dangerous to society, in general, because you both drive."

"Hey, I didn't come here to be lectured about my drinking habits!" Vince tried to bark. The words came out slurred and with less than potent force.

"I'm sure you didn't. Dr. Kronenberg was also a cocky, self-important, aggressive man, who got more aggressive as he drank. It showed clearly when he got behind the wheel of his Mercedes. A gigantic, silver 400SE. Which is how he came to dent the driver's door of a car he wanted out of his way. Stove the door in and zoomed past."

A warning bell went off in Vince's head. This lecture was going somewhere he knew he wouldn't like. Damn the rest of the hour. He wanted out. He tried to push himself off the couch, got halfway up, and collapsed back.

"Amazing what a couple little pills can accomplish," the man seated at the desk said. "I'm so glad you insisted on taking two. You're mighty big, Vince." He pushed himself off the desk and moved his bow-legged body swiftly to the trolley, grabbing an unopened bottle of Perrier in his right hand.

Vince struggled again, aided by the adrenaline squirting into his bloodstream from a million little pockets. This time he made it to his feet. A moment later, he was down flat on the carpet, felled by a crisply delivered whack of the Perrier bottle against his forehead.

The psychiatrist barked, "Kronenberg hit my door; you took off my bumper, with the ridiculous steel cage on the front of that tank you call a truck. Ripped it off and kept right on going. Hit and run."

"I remember," Vince said, trying to master the bump on his head and the drugs and panic in his veins. "You pulled ten feet past the stop sign. Right into the street. It was your fault. There was no way I was gonna stop, though. Nearly midnight. Nobody else at that intersection as a witness. The media would have had a field day with me."

"Because you were drinking, Vince," the little man said, suddenly calm. Then, in a nearly unintelligible shriek that made the veins pop out on both sides of his scrawny neck, "And I was not ten feet past the stop sign! I am an excellent driver!" He spun around, rushed to the far side of the desk, and yanked open the top drawer. From it, he pulled a tire iron and a child's jump rope capped on either side by red-enameled wooden handles. He labored to regain control, swallowing several times, as if to eat his agitation. "The same damned thing with Kronenberg. He sees me signaling to pull into the fast lane, but he's already made up his mind to pass me. Big man in a big car. Get out of his way. Lays on the horn and the gas pedal at the same time. Never mind I'm in front of him. Bam! And then he flies on past. But not before I get his license number. Just like I got yours."

Vince set both his knees on the carpet, aligning himself with the inner door. He knew it would take every bit of his concentration to overcome the drugs, but once he got going his size and strength would be enough to get him to the outer door. Then it would depend on whether or not this madman had locked them in. He had to keep the guy answering questions, give his body time to pump out lots more adrenaline.

"So, you got into my condo. Drugged my bourbon."

"That's right. Had to get into your condo several times. First, I bugged every room. You picked a bad victim to fuck with, Vince. I make my living in the commercial security business. Locks. Closed-circuit cameras. Recently expanded into the high-tech stuff. Build computer firewalls and so forth. Got access to every computer record in the world on you.'

"And did you find a string of DUIs with lots of Motor Vehicle Departments?"

"No. Of course not. You're a hit-and-run expert. You make sure you're not arrested. That's why I have to take the law into my own hands, Mr. Football Hero. Just like I did with Kronenberg. I hope you appreciate all the time and care I took. Had to break into Kronenberg's office and get his stationery. Had to call the receptionist here today and cancel your appointment, a few minutes after you made the call. Then break in at 5:30 and be all set up by 6:00."

"How did you disguise your voice to sound like Kronenberg's?"

"Computer. They have these wonderful wave generators now that can make anybody sound like a woman, a child – even a macho man like you."

Vince's output signals were definitely being scrambled, but his hearing was perfect. The stereo sense of his ears told him that the man was standing directly behind him and not more than a couple feet back. Vince grappled with his memory for those half-dozen karate lessons he had taken in the seventies to be able to endorse that academy. He rocked his weight onto his hands, drew up his right leg and kicked upward and back to the limit of his diminished powers.

Air whooshed from the man's lungs as Vince's foot connected with his groin. He double over so quickly that his glasses popped off the bridge of his nose. The tire iron and jump rope fell from his hands as he clutched at his testicles.

A soon as Vince lurched to his feet, he tottered around and threw the Perrier bottle at the man's face. It was a bullet, sailing in a tight spiral, but it was not delivered on the numbers. Instead, it struck the desk and exploded in a blossom of natural carbonation. Vince reoriented himself and staggered past the tea trolley to the doorway and into the outer office, where he collided with the receptionist's desk, rebounded and fought for several seconds to maintain his balance. He found the blurred rectangle of the outer door and lumbered toward it. His hand found the doorknob.

The tire iron drove into the side of Vince's left knee, the force of the blow shattering bone and cartilage. Vince toppled like a mighty tree. His arms thrust out in barely enough time to shield his face from the oak door. He had never felt such agony, and only the dulling of the drug kept him from passing out.

"Now you know what Namath felt like. You shoulda finished me off in the other room, Vince," the little man gasped, in a voice choked with both pain and rage. "Just like you shoulda finished off the 49ers, even though you were two touchdowns ahead. You don't have the killer instinct. Neither do I. But you're a killer anyway. Sooner or later, you'd run some child over with that big toy of yours. Or a mother. So I have to make myself into a killer to protect society. The police don't. Even MADD can't. It's up to decent citizens like me. I thought about just leaving you to face Kronenberg's murder, but you'd beat it. Thanks to the soulless lawyers, you rich people always win. And then you'd be out on the highway again."

The tire iron fell to the carpet. The jump rope came over Vince's head, looped once around his neck, and tightened. It would have been easier to have simply crushed his skull, as he had with Kronenberg, but he didn't want blood all over an innocent psychiatrist's office. So he pulled with all his strength. Eventually, the clawing fingers lost their strength, the whipping back and forth subsided. He held tight for three full minutes after Martelli ceased struggling. Then he let go, collapsed into one of the Bauhaus chairs and surveyed his work through squinting eyes. There was no joy left in his expression. He had tortured Martelli precisely as much as he thought he was owed for his own pain and suffering. The sportscaster's death was merely preventative justice, nothing to gloat over. Now all that remained was cleaning up the office and getting the huge body out of the building unseen.

He returned to the inner office and groped around the carpet until he found his spectacles. Once they were back on his face, he felt much more in control. He turned out the inner office lights, not wanting any witness outside the building to register that the office was being used. More than enough light poured in from the reception area and from the tall floodlights in the parking lot. From his jacket pocket he pulled a handkerchief, preparing to wipe the office clean of prints from back to front. He moved to the picture window, to see how many cars remained in the parking lot.

Two stories below, the eighty asphalt spaces held just three vehicles: a late-model Lincoln Continental; Vince's prized Land Cruiser; a white panel van with the legend "Dave's Total Security Systems" neatly stenciled on its side. As he scanned the lot, Dave saw the taillights of the Lincoln come on, then glow bright red as the car backed up. And backed up. And backed up. Directly into the corner of Dave's van. Smashing out both the tail and parking lights.

As Dave watched in speechless shock, the Lincoln pulled forward five feet. A fat man in a dark suit waddled back to survey the damage. He looked first at his car, then at the van, then at the deserted parking lot, and finally at the office building. Satisfied that no one had seen the accident, he climbed back into his car.

"Son of a bitch!" Dave screamed. He rushed to the telescope and trained it down on the Lincoln, which had already begun to turn. The rear license plate came clearly visible in the telescope's focus. ARBITR8. On his way in, Dave had noted the law office on the first floor.

"Not again!" Dave wailed. And this time by a lawyer. His shoulders slumped. He had not even finished cleaning up after his latest administration of justice, and another bastard had steered his way into the retribution line.

Dave slowly straightened up. He looked at the handkerchief in his hand. Well, there was nothing to do but go on. It was God's will – and he was God's avenging angel. Tomorrow morning, he'd have to cancel the vacation to Cancun and begin the tedious process of learning every detail about Mr. ARBITR8. Dave shook his head, sighed and began dusting.

Shedding Light on
the Black Forest
(From *100 Wicked Witch Tales*)

You've heard the tale; I know you have. But you've heard it wrong. I can set the record straight; I was there when it happened.

They Germanized the alleged witch's name when they spread the story. Rosina Boccafine was of pure Sicilian stock – the old crone capital of the Western world. You know what I mean. The women turn ancient at fifty. Hair kinky and gray as a Brillo pad. Thick Mediterranean skin, fully wrinkled after only five decades. Brown half-circles under eyes shining like polished coal. Most of their teeth missing. Errant hairs poking out from under their noses and chins. And, of course, in that part of the world, every woman wears nothing but black once she becomes a widow. An image frightening enough in its totality. Yet Rosina managed to exceed the stereotype. She sported a large wart on her left nostril. She was also stooped to the point of hunchback from a lifetime of menial work. Finally, her voice sounded like a rusty-hinged barn door on a windy day. Such an easy target for the label of witch.

With the true gall of the pot calling the kettle black, her perpetually sinning neighbor wives bruited it about that Signora Boccafine had murdered her husband of twenty-eight years, Signore Alfredo Boccafine. The simple truth was that what had first attracted Alfredo to Rosina was also what killed him. If she could be said to be a sorceress in any sense of the term, it was in the creation of food – both cooked and baked. Despite nearly thirty years of consuming his wife's miraculous bracciole, Alfredo once neglected to remove one of the toothpicks. Toothpick and unrolling beef lodged in his throat. Powdered cheese tumbled into his windpipe, and the spices swelled his vocal cords shut. *Addio, Alfredo.*

Rosina had never had children of her own. Perhaps she had never wanted them. She was not the most patient or forbearing of women. But children she got aplenty after Alfredo's death. She couldn't work her husband's farmland by herself, so she sold it. She should have used the money to open a bakery in some city. But she had heard tell that land was dirt cheap near Lindau, just above Switzerland. The tract she bought was, in fact, half a day's walk from Lindau, through the infamous Black Forest, along little more than a wolf path. One needed a compass to find one's way in or out. Which made it a virtual prison for those unfamiliar with the forest – and made it a perfect location for a school for difficult children…another idea suggested to Rosina that again, unfortunately, she latched onto.

Lindau is only a day's ride on horseback to the borders of France, Austria and Lichtenstein, as well as parts of Switzerland. In no time at all, word spread that Widow Boccafine had opened a place she benignly called "The Cottage", where embarrassments to well-heeled families could be stuck until age drained some of the vinegar out of them. That is how I, Jean-Claude Facheux, scion of the vintner family, ended up in the middle of the

Schwarzwald. And that is also how Margaretha and Johann got there, too. Chance and family deprivations played no part.

When the Holzhackers arrived, she was twelve and he was eight. They told us, simply, that their mother had died and that their incarceration at The Cottage was a result of a wicked stepmother. Through my extensive research and the benefit of the years' distance from the incident, I can tell you that their mother had not just died; she had been killed. The official report was that she had been murdered in her own kitchen by a vagrant, stabbed sixteen times in the back with a kitchen knife (which had not been recovered). The vagrant (a sad fellow with a long history of insanity) had been hanged by the outraged neighbors before the law could question him. The father, Heinrich, had married just six months later. No one could blame him. He had a thriving lumber supply business to run. He needed a housekeeper and mother for his children. His second wife, Hanna, was only seventeen but had married Heinrich in spite of the chasm between their ages and his children's reputations. She no doubt figured that they would both be out of the house soon enough, and if she gritted her teeth hard she'd be set for life.

But then more light was shed upon the murder. Being of true Teutonic stock, Hanna scrubbed the floors every day, which is how she came upon the loose floorboard in Johann's room.

And the blood-stained missing kitchen knife beneath it.

Looking at the exquisitely beautiful Margaretha and her innocent brother, Heinrich couldn't deal with the truth staring him in the face. In exchange for Hanna never mentioning her discovery again, he promised to pack Margaretha and Johann off to The Cottage.

The eight of us (ranging in age from seven to twelve) who had already been enrolled at The Cottage before Greta and Johann arrived were a bad lot. Typical antics had included filling shoes with horse manure, stealing money from parents' purses, setting fires, cheating at tests, throwing temper tantrums of monumental proportions, putting pins in infants' diapers, and tying junk to dogs' tails. The combined mayhem we attempted was enough to turn any woman into a figurative witch, and naturally we did not instantly change our natures just because we had come to The Cottage. Every day, Rosina's cackling voice sounded shrilly through the forest, and many a birch tree was stripped clean of branches for punishment. In retrospect, it's easy to see how Greta convinced us the woman was in league with the devil. But we were lambs compared to the Holzhacker children. Greta's long, blonde hair and lake-blue eyes made instant captives of the older boys, myself counted among them. But this was not good enough for Greta. The day she moved in, she shared with us two stories of the Holzhacker children's accomplishments, tales intended to show us that their new leadership had better remain unchallenged. Greta, it seemed, had guaranteed herself a lively twelfth birthday party by spiking the punch with mandrake root. Her guests had danced, sung and chattered like ones possessed until they all collapsed from exhaustion. Johann's proudest moment was tumbling a priest from his donkey with a stone from his slingshot, the most dignified of victims who had been knocked unconscious by one of the smooth, silvery stones he kept in his pockets for ammunition. The mention of smooth, silver stones should jostle your memory as an element of this affair. That is because the most accomplished of liars always sew in rags of real life to make the patchwork quilt of their fantastic tales look all the more true.

As I said, Rosina Boccafine was sorely vexed, night and day, by our antics. But she knew she had one advantage that could cow the worst among us: her baking delights. Anyone caught misbehaving would be denied her delicious cookies and pastries. Those caught breaking the fundamental rules were denied the main course, as well, and given only bread and water. It usually worked with the original eight of us, because we were only mischievous and not evil; we concerned ourselves with the pure fun of a misdeed and not especially in making sure our tracks were covered. Not so with the Holzhackers. Their plan was twofold: to drive the woman insane with bedevilments and to convince us she nightly rode that broom she employed so assiduously by day. Greta and Johann spent every spare hour collecting the most gruesome manner of insects to plant in Signora Boccafine's bedclothes. Her snuff was lightly peppered. They sawed another half-inch off her cane every few days. They rubbed a fine layer of lard across her spectacles, to make her believe her eyesight was rapidly failing. Always without being caught. Meantime, they had us quaking in our clogs by wondering aloud how a woman living alone in the middle of the forest, never visited by hunters or butchers, could make beef goulash. Parents were not expecting any of us back, Greta declared. And even though we had witnessed the disappearance of none of our number, she added, it was only a matter of time.

But even the truly wicked slip up now and then. One day, Rosina's dog died in a ball of flame. Despite a frantic scrubbing in lye soap, Johann's hands still held the telltale odor of kerosene. The dog's pen, now empty, became Johann's permanent home. But he was still well fed. The same day as the dog was cremated, Rosina's spectacles disappeared. She was quite nearsighted and was reduced to feeling the fat on Johann's arm each day to be sure that he was not wasting away on a hunger strike. The daily act was not lost on the young Miss Holzhacker, who pointed it out to all of us. On the fatal day prior to the incident, she told us all that she had awakened the night before and looked out the window to see Signora Boccafine conferring with a goat who stood on its two hind legs. She had worn her usual black clothing and held her broom, but she also wore a pointed hat. She had gestured to the nearly full moon and then to the kennel where Johann Holzhacker slept. More than one bed was wet the next morning.

Each of us had particular chores around The Cottage, skills that would serve us in later life. Mine was milking the cows and taking them to and from pasture. The girls all had indoor chores. Greta's was helping with the baking. She had feigned a dull wit around Signora Boccafine since she arrived.

Little did we know how well her ruse would serve her.

Clans throughout Europe are, to my way of thinking, all rather brutal. My people, for example, thought nothing of burning the Maid of Orleans alive at the stake. But the Germans have a special cruelty in their souls. It would never have occurred to a Facheux, using the ruse of stupidity, to shove an old woman into an oven and then latch the door. Her screams still echo in my head.

Margaretha – who we sometimes called "Greta" but insisted she be called "Gretel" to make herself seem sweeter – managed to lead us out of the deep woods. All the while we walked, she coached us in what to say. While her brother shot birds out of the trees with his smooth, silver stones, she warned us that, given our collective reputations, if we did not all tell the same exaggerated tale, the grownups of Lindau would suspect us of group murder. I frankly did not think that people in their thirties and forties would buy it – particularly the part about some of us having been turned into large gingerbread cookies. But this is, after all, a dark age in Europe and not the enlightened times of the ancient Greeks. Black cats die as soon as they are born, and the mice and rats run rampant in the streets.

Johann Holzhacker, or Hansel as his sister called him, died at the ripe old age of seventeen in an inn brawl with college students. He may have traded his slingshot prematurely for a knife. It proved a good two feet shorter than the freshman's rapier.

Greta, I hear, has used her great wit and beauty to ensnare the heart of a king. A widower, it turns out. The only trouble is that the king loves his only daughter equally. In contrast to Greta, the girl's hair is as black as a window frame, her lips as red as blood and her skin as white as snow. I fear justly for the girl and believe it is only a matter of time before her life will be cut short. I pray that Greta the Witch should come to the horrible end she deserves. But such justice, it seems, is meted out only in fairy tales.

The Shadow Knows
(From *Monsters From Memphis*)

Mahoney is my name. I run a detective agency. Don't expect Mike Hammer or Sam Spade. I'm an unspectacular guy and, despite what the literary liars feed you, I'm in an unspectacular line of work. Most of the time. Lots of folks cheating but resenting it if their spouses do the same; people getting themselves intentionally lost; embezzlers; some arsonists and insurance frauds; vanished college loan cheats; once in a blue moon a blackmailing or kidnapping. I'm paid to pull back the blankets, shine the light on the darkness, find the path through the maze. My ancestors built this nation's canals with picks and shovels; when I dig, my hands only get figuratively dirty.

The other half of the business is my wife, Siobhan. We came from the Aulde Sod eleven years ago. Settled in Memphis because of the sizable Irish population. Some of our long-departed relatives arrived shortly before the War of Northern Aggression. The gene pool was adventurous enough to cross the Atlantic Ocean, you see, but lazy enough to call the westward advance quits when they had to get themselves across the formidable Mississippi River. That pretty much sums me up, too: motivated enough to get off my butt but ready to sit back down if it gets too formidable. When that happens, it usually takes Siobhan to give me a swift verbal kick in the arse to convince me to finish the job. She holds down the office, pays the bills – but, most importantly, does seventy percent of the "legwork" with the modern tools of the trade: computers, the internet, the phone, the fax machine, the databanks, the directories.

You're wondering why I'm here spilling my guts to you instead of at work in Memphis. No, I'm not on vacation. It has to do with a case. I case I already solved.

It began with a call from Irene Scully. You might remember her as Irene Warne. Miss Memphis, 1981. Should have been Miss Tennessee except that her only talent was her looks. Her flaming baton twirling act was a disaster. Irene was the wife of Justice Owen Meriweather Scully III, former senior partner of Scully & Burke, Attorneys at Law, and considerably senior partner in his marriage. Owen and Irene had separated, but both refused to move out of the mansion, possession being nine-tenths of the law. Shortly after the agreement of irreconcilable differences, the 52-year-old Owen had taken up jogging and was out for hours at a time. Irene might have bought the sudden health kick except that Owen wasn't losing any weight. And the Nike joggers still had all their tread after three weeks. There's not a woman alive, Irene included, dumb enough to miss what that meant. She contacted me about following him. What we in the profession call "shadowing." I was already on a case, but I promised to start the next night. One night too late as it turned out. Owen Scully left the house at 8:25 p.m. and never returned.

Irene hired me anyway. She was afraid the police and the insurance company would think she had figured out a way not to have to divide the community property. One conversation with Irene, and the police and policy investigator would drop any suspicions that she could mastermind a clean killing. But I was not above cashing in on some of that community property.

My first visit was to the police station. I hunted down my pal, Detective Frances DePiano. If anyone in Memphis leads a cinema noir life, it's Frank. And yet he, who should know better than anyone else in town, has sold himself on the romance of the private eye. It's not in my self-interest to disabuse him. I occasionally leave a case of Ruffino Chianti in his back seat as thanks for the inside information he feeds me.

I officially informed Frank on Irene's behalf of Justice Scully's disappearance.

"Not everyone on the force knows His Honor," Frank said, checking the blotter. "Nope. No John Does last night. But we have had a rash of disappearances lately, each time followed by a body."

I asked him what number constituted a rash.

"Three."

I asked in how much time.

"Three weeks. Every Sunday, like clockwork, somebody disappears. Every Wednesday night they die."

He had my undivided attention. I wondered aloud why I hadn't heard about it.

"Well, several reasons," Frank answered. "They were all black. One from the Riverview Park area, one from near Bellevue Park, one from just east of Glenview Park. Poorest parts of town.

None could afford to be your client. Not even important enough to rate the front of the newspaper."

I guessed the police were after a serial killer.

"Nah. Much weirder than that. Sunday night the disappearance. Monday, Tuesday or Wednesday night they're seen. But never in their usual haunts. In fact, in haunts they wouldn't be caught dead in. We learn about this after the fact. Some time on Thursday the corpse is found. But it died on Wednesday night."

And why couldn't it be the work of a serial killer I wanted to know.

"Because the 'killer' is some kind of disease. The pathology boys say that if it is infectious the person transmitting it would have to do more than kiss somebody to give it to them. As far as we can tell, none of the victims knew the others existed. The doctors haven't figured it out, but it seems more like cancer than anything else. It eats away parts of their brains and parts of their hearts. That's the other reason you haven't heard anything: We don't want to start a panic over a disease that only one person a week contracts. Nobody in the media has noticed the pattern, so we're happy to sit on it. At least for the time being."

I pumped DePiano for specifics on 'the haunts they wouldn't be caught dead in' angle.

"Okay. The first one was named Sammy Morris. Owned an auto junkyard down by the river. Nickname was Tank. Big, macho guy. Five kids by three different women. But on the Tuesday night after his disappearance he's dressed like a transvestite and parading his stuff in The Pink Lady.

"The second was a woman. LaTrina Miles. Ran a custodial business. Her people cleaned a dozen office firms downtown. She musta bid too low, 'cause she lived on Greenwood. Disappears three Sundays ago. Who-the-hell knows where she hid herself all Monday and Tuesday day. But Tuesday late afternoon she's at her bank just as they're closing, looking hale and hearty and demanding to get into her deposit box. The employee points to the clock, tells her the vault is locked until morning and suggests that she come back then. Ms. Miles starts screaming, puts the woman into a hammer lock and demands she open the vault. Two other employees had to come to her rescue. Ms. Miles flees on foot. She does not return the next morning. Or afternoon. So maybe I'm stretching the point saying she wouldn't be caught dead there, but once she went berserk she didn't return. And then she literally was caught dead.

"The third one's Eddie Pendleton. He managed the apartment house on South Parkway with the Greek statues out front. You know: the one we call the Venus de Milo Arms. A true homey. Always drove his LeBaron with gangsta rap blasting. But when he's found on Thursday morning, he's dressed in a rented tuxedo with a stub for the previous night's Memphis Symphony in one pocket. We checked with the holders of the seats on either side. He was definitely at the concert and apparently loving every minute of it. Elgar, Delius and Vaughn-Williams, ferchrissake! Not exactly his haunt, or what?

"I'd say Justice Scully's safe," Frank concluded. "He's the wrong color and living in the right part of town."

I didn't feel as optimistic. He had disappeared on a Sunday night.

"Strange shit," DePiano added. "We've got plainclothesmen patrolling the 'poor peoples' parks, but I'll be damned if I know what we're looking for."

I thanked Frank for the background and headed for the Venus de Milo Arms, equally damned if I knew what I was looking for. Irene Scully had agreed to pick up expenses regardless, so I bribed the temporary manager to let me into Eddie Pendleton's digs. Fortunately, Eddie had no relatives living in Memphis, or the vultures would definitely have picked the apartment clean.

I was frankly flabbergasted. the putative lover of gangsta rap had a living room filled with classical records and CDs. And the stuff he played it on didn't come out of Circuit City. The amplifier, tuner, turntable, CD player and other assorted toys were the kind of quality advertised in *Audiophile*. If they were mountains, they would have been Everest/K2 class. Had to be an easy ten thousand bucks of equipment. But no speakers. Studio pro headphones only. Nobody in the Armless Arms was hearing this music except Eddie. And another ten thousand worth of wax and disk. All concealed behind cabinet doors. Out of view of guests. Other than the bizarre dichotomy between public and private listening tastes, Eddie's pad revealed nothing to shed light on his "disease" or disappearance. I spoke with three of the tenants.

Eddie was well liked. Did his best to see that the apartment house was neat and respectable, himself being the living example.

I waited until nightfall and tried to gain entrance to Sammy Morris's junkyard, but the place was very well lit, the chain-link fence was topped by concertina razor wire, and a pair of famished-looking Dobermans patrolled on the inside. Like I said: I'm ready to sit back down if it gets too formidable. Instead, I discovered two of Sammy's girlfriends. One corroborated the other. Sammy lived simply inside the junkyard, but he took excellent care of his women and kids. When I asked if he had any effeminate tendencies, one laughed in my face. The other one slapped my face. They had never heard of Eddie Pendleton or LaTrina Miles.

When I couldn't convince the two nieces who lived with LaTrina to talk with me or let me into her duplex, I waited until they were out and made a keyless entry through her back door. Again, nothing. The place was tastefully done. The furniture was better than Walmart quality. Yet not on the level I expected for a woman who had six people in her employ.

I have a friend in the State Department of Revenue. She works in the Alcoholic Beverage Commission, but nobody throughout Revenue would deny data access if they thought it was official business. I asked her to see if Inheritance Tax had any info yet on LaTrina Miles's estate. The bank had reported on the inventory of the contents of the safe deposit box. It held a passport that had entry stamps from a dozen countries. It also had

$37,000 in neatly banded hundred-dollar bills. Suddenly, instead of thinking that Ms. Miles had seriously undercharged for her custodial services, I was thinking she had seriously overcharged. When I called one of her nieces, posing as her travel agent, the woman had no idea her aunt went anywhere except "to some religious retreat every year for two weeks."

Siobhan worked her armchair wizardry in getting LaTrina's custodial rates. The woman charged about ten percent below average. Enough to win just about any client she wanted to. Her peoples' work was rated high. No complaints.

LaTrina had lots of secret money for travel. Eddie blew thousands he shouldn't have had on music. Sammy was generous to three women and five kids via a third-rate junkyard. Wealth was a hell of a common denominator for three supposedly poor people who had died of an exotic disease. It didn't figure at all.

I was working my weary way home on Tuesday night, having vainly interrogated Irene as to any secret money deals her husband may have had cooking, when I heard on the police scanner that Martin "The Thumb" O'Malley had just been blown away getting into his car. O'Malley was a Memphis racketeer who had beaten two indictments for murder. The next morning, Frank DePiano calls me and says that Solly Bosco had also met his maker later that same night. Solly was a hood who had survived various raps for narcotics trafficking and was also suspected of liquidating local competitors. The weapon that ventilated both wise guys was a .45. Maybe the same weapon. But

Forensics wouldn't let Frank know by closing time. That was a Wednesday.

Now, if I was a totally honest guy, I would have shared what I knew with Detective DePiano. But I wanted that reward for locating Judge Scully real bad. I figured I'd get square with Frank by pulling in one of the Sunday Night Missing alive. One thing I knew was that Martin O'Malley and Solly Bosco had both come up in front of Judge Scully's bench and had literally gotten away with murder. Scully was a hanging judge. He had done what he could within the limits of the law to help the prosecution, but shoddy police work and idiot juries had confounded him.

One other major piece of scum had evaded Judge Scully's legal wrath. The bottom feeder had tried his hand at every illegal act there was, including "wet jobs." His name was Lenzy Rust. Lenzy lived in the Orange Mound district, in one of its grandest houses (which is not saying all that much.) Word was he kept his BMW locked up inside a windowless garage and used a remote-control ignition to start the car. He had not stayed alive by luck.

I waited until dusk on Wednesday to drive into Orange Mound. In daylight, I'd have looked like a marshmallow in a licorice factory. Besides, from the little I had learned, I knew that nothing would happen until the sun sank beyond the Mississippi. I spotted a cozy nook across the street from Rust's place to stand guard. A shoulder harness was strapped under my jacket, cradling my Smith & Wesson New Century. I used the damn gun so seldom, I had cleaned it and practiced with it out at the local target range that afternoon.

Lenzy was a creature of the night. Like a cockroach. The door didn't crank up until after 11:00 p.m. Lenzy emerged from the house's side exit, dressed in "What a Target!" white. He had one hand stuck in his pocket. Before he reached the garage, the BMW's engine purred to life. The blur of white was in the driver's seat before you could say, "Ashes to ashes, dust to dust/where there's a scratch, you'll find Rust." I'm no poet, but I had had plenty of time to kill, so I dreamed up a few bad epithets for Lenzy's headstone. I was that certain he was about to meet the same fate as Martin O'Malley and Solly Bosco. I could have prevented his passing, I suppose, but I'm a better citizen than that.

So I watched Owen Scully materialize out of the shadows of Lenzy Rust's property, put a bullet into each of the BMW's driver-side tires, then aim a third into the driver's window. I was surprised to see the glass crack but not shatter. But Judge Scully was not. As Rust reversed the transmission to mash his attacker into the side of his house, Scully calmly sidestepped and, with his left hand, smashed a brick into the bulletproof window. It crunched in enough to make a silver-dollar-sized hole. A moment after the BMW's fender took out three courses of aluminum siding, Scully pressed the muzzle of his automatic to the hole and pumped the remaining four shots into his victim.

The car horn started blowing. I stepped out of my own shadows and yelled out over the noise for Judge Scully to put up his hands. My right hand was already up, pointing my .44 at him. He blinked but clearly was not so astonished that he was about to meekly obey me. Instead, he turned and ran down the driveway. I could have nailed him in the back, but I was not about to commit murder for what Irene Scully was paying. I was especially not eager to murder somebody who, if he was indeed like the three before him, would be dead by dawn anyway. Then there's the fact that live men generally give better explanations than dead ones. The Memphis police would no doubt be very grateful to me if I could focus a floodlight on the phenomenon of the Sunday Night Missing.

I gave chase. My purpose was to keep Owen Scully in sight, not to apprehend him myself. I didn't think it would be too difficult. He was, after all, almost twenty years older and fifty pounds heavier than me. With my free hand, I used my cellphone and pressed 911 while I ran. The Memphis cops are generally not bad when it comes to response time. I figured within five minutes it would all be over. While I was talking with the dispatcher, Scully jogged across a major thoroughfare and turned at the sidewalk. I was between two parked cars on the opposite side of the street when something told me to duck. A moment later, three hunks of hot lead remodeled the car to my right. Scully had at least one spare clip on him.

I finished the call in a tight squat. By the time I risked a peek, the judge had vanished. In spite of the danger, I couldn't let him get away. He hadn't re-crossed the street, so he had either gone east or west with the sidewalk, or north into a nearby alley. I took the alley. Slowly. With Smith & Wesson in front of me. The corridor made a sharp left turn. I hugged the dark wall and inched forward. When I looked around the corner, I saw Judge Scully lying face up under a utility pole lamp. Gliding away from the body on the far wall was the full-size shadow of a man. I dared the light and, with my weapon cocked and raised, called out for whoever was retreating to halt. The shadow continued along the wall and disappeared into inky blackness. I strained to see the person who had created it, but to me the other end of the alley looked totally empty. Like some giant monster's maw yawning open.

I glanced at Owen Scully. His maw was definitely yawning open. Fresh blood coated his teeth and lips. His eyes were wide open and bulging, as though his last seconds had been extremely painful. Just beyond his right hand lay a Colt automatic.

Traffic whizzed by out on the thoroughfare, but the alley lay as silent as Scully. It invited me forward. Against my better judgment, I rushed into the blackness. I wanted at least a glimpse at the owner of the shadow. I jinked and darted down the long, narrow space, like a pinball in a frenzied game. Once inside the darkness, I saw that the alley ended not far beyond. Dead ended. Only one door and two heavily barred windows back there. The door was sheathed in metal and locked. I figured if it had been opened within the past minute, I would have heard some creaking. I heard nothing. I looked up. No fire escape. I looked down. A sewer grate along the alley curb but no manhole cover in the asphalt. As I stood in the darkness doing a slow

360, I heard the approaching wail of a police siren. I jogged back along the alley and out into the street to flag them down. Fortunately, I knew one of the cops, so the tedious crap of identifying and exonerating myself was dispensed with.

By five o'clock on Thursday, I had two bits of information. The first was the ironic fact that the Colt that had blown away O'Malley, Bosco and Rust had been ostensibly used by Lenzy Rust in committing a murder three years earlier. It had vanished from the evidence cage on the day Rust had been acquitted. The other news was the official report on Judge Scully's demise. Same cause of death as the previous three Sunday Night Missing. Parts of the brain and heart eaten away. Tears in the tissue of his lungs and esophagus. Massive bleeding that would have been a lot more messy except that death came within seconds. When I told Frank DePiano about the shadow figure, he dismissed it as temporary hysteria. Probably my own shadow from another light behind me. I went back to the alley that night to check it out. There was no other light.

Irene Scully paid me my out-of-pocket and per diem, but she held to her deal of no big payoff unless Owen came back home alive. Fair enough. That wasn't bothering me half as much as the whole incident in the alley. Someone other than me had made that shadow and then vanished. Houdini couldn't have done better. I had stood on a New York City sidewalk for half an hour when I first got to the U.S., until I figured out how Three-Card Monte was done. I wasn't going to walk away from this either until I understood it.

I had the chance for a week-long dock surveillance right after Judge Scully died, but I turned it down. It was across the river and would have made chasing the next Sunday Night Missing impossible. Sunday found me and my Smith & Wesson strolling through the sylvan shadows of Tobey Park. It's located between Christian Brothers College and the very tony Chickasaw Gardens bedroom community. Judge Scully had lived in Chickasaw Gardens, but his wallet had been found in the grass at the edge of a parking lot for the Mid-South Fairgrounds. Not in a park. Which told me two things. The first was that whatever had overtaken the four victims had chosen parks not because they were parks but rather because they were dimly lit and sparsely peopled at night. The fairgrounds were not in use and quite dark and deserted that time of year. That was probably the reason Owen Scully had picked that particular area. He had walked the safe distance from home and was picked up by his girlfriend and driven to their love nest. The second thing was that if you had a map of Memphis, you could draw a ruler-straight line through Riverview, Bellevue and Glenview Parks, and right up to the Fairgrounds. Whatever it was that had infected the four victims had done so along a precisely southwest to northeast course and was now halfway across the city, in its very heart. The next isolated spot on the extended line was Tobey Park.

The one thing I did not want was to be the next victim. As I walked, I turned often and watched over both shoulders. I had practiced enough to know that my revolver could be in my hand in two seconds flat. I had envisioned a mad scientist skulking through Memphis's dimly lit and isolated areas on his night off, hypodermic in hand, seeking out guinea pigs for his latest formula. My vision did not put him in a white lab coat, easy to spot.

There were even fewer people out that night than I expected. One was a majestically white-haired priest, dressed in a black cassock and sitting on one of the park benches – no doubt on a constitutional from Christian Brothers, a block away. I dipped my head in deference to him, but he did not see me – seemingly lost in thought with his eyes focused at infinity. I made a perambulation of the park's outer path, spotting nothing out of the ordinary. Then I was back at the priest's bench. The priest was no longer there. But his cassock was. It lay on the grass behind the bench, trailed out toward the bushes.

I had brought a flashlight with me. It wasn't the general variety but rather the krypton type. If our Revolutionary War patriots had used one in Boston's North Church, they could have signaled minutemen in Providence. I plunged into the vegetation, swinging the powerful beam back and forth. Far ahead of me was the priest, lurching through the undergrowth. He turned when the light hit him. He lifted his arms to ward off the blinding beam and gave forth an inhuman roar. Since I was within fifty feet of him, I chanced balancing the flashlight in the crotch of a tree and circled swiftly and silently to his right. Just as I was nearly upon him, he rushed in my direction. I sidestepped and caught him behind the left ear with the muzzle of my revolver. He fell hard. This one was not slipping away from me.

I sat on the old man's back. As quickly as I could, I took off my belt and secured his hands behind him. Then I removed his belt and hog-tied his legs, pulling his feet up close to his hands. By the time I returned with the flashlight, he was regaining consciousness. He rolled over and stared up at me. With eyebrows raised in a look of surprise.

"You again?" he exclaimed. "I should have killed you last week."

I am sure my look of surprise greatly outdid his.

"You're the shadow I saw in the alley," I said.

He struggled vainly against the belts. "That's right."

I leaned against a tree for much-needed support. "It was a dead end. How did you get out?"

"I went down into the sewer."

"But how could you fit?"

"I can fit through a keyhole if I choose," the priest answered. "Turn that light away! It hurts me."

Despite the strangeness of his words, I obliged. Then he laughed. "I thought you understood. I've given you too much credit."

Suddenly, I did know. "You are the shadow in the alley! Nothing more."

The priest rolled over, so that his face was turned from the light. "I'm sure I'm more than that. But I must look so to humans. Close enough so that I can glide up to your mouths and noses and crawl in without you becoming suspicious. I truthfully don't know what I look like."

"What are you?" I asked, once I had recovered my voice.

"I have very little idea. I don't know how I began or where. My guess is not long ago and somewhere near the Mississippi River."

"You're damned articulate for something that began not long ago. Do you understand the word 'articulate'?"

"Of course. I understand whatever Tank Morris, LaTrina Miles, Eddie Pendleton and Owen Scully understood. I have all their memories inside me."

I kept my revolver raised and walked around to look at the priest's face. "You understand that you eventually kill those you invade, don't you?"

"Yes."

"Why do you do it?"

"Because the nearest thing I can compare myself to is a computer diskette. I'm filled with memories, but I can't use them unless I get myself inside a human head. The mind acts like a microprocessor for me. Outside on my own, I operate on simple instinct. I crave completion. I can only be without it for four days. Then I have to get inside someone."

"Unfortunately, you kill them after three days," I pointed out. "Eat away parts of their brains and hearts."

"Yes. I can feel it happening. When the heart starts to go wild, I force my way out again and seek dark water."

Then I understood the pattern of its victim taking. The Memphis sewer and storm drain systems empty to the north into the Wolf River and to the south into Nonconnah Creek. One large drain runs southwest, under the Fairgrounds, Glenview, Belleview, and Riverview Parks. One runs northwest, under Robert Howze Park, the Chickasaw Country Club and Gaisman Park. Both begin by draining Tobey Park. It was a creature of water and of darkness. Even when it was inside a human body, it couldn't abide sunlight. That was why the victims had never been seen during full daylight. They probably holed up in the storm drains until dusk.

"If you have only a simple nervous system yourself," I said, "how do you choose your victims?"

"By smell," it answered without reflection.

"Smell," I repeated. "Do humans give off a particular smell to you?"

"Yes. But not all humans. Only a certain kind."

I knew it couldn't mean black persons, because Owen Scully and the priest were white. I knew it couldn't mean old, because Sammy Morris and LaTrina were not even thirty.

"Can you define the kind?" I asked.

"Hypocrites," it answered. "Again, you look surprised. Perhaps you can't smell them, but I can. Not when I'm inside a human body, you see. But outside, it's like beer to a slug. Do you want me to prove it?"

I admitted I did.

"Tank Morris claimed he owned a completely legitimate junkyard. But a lot of his inventory came from a chop shop he ran, four blocks away. If he was just selling stolen hubcaps, he might have lived. LaTrina Miles had her employees go through wastebaskets, drawers, file cabinets – locked and unlocked – even into computers, digging for stuff she could sell to the competition. She was very clever about it. Never once arrested. She cleaned up all right. Eddie Pendleton was so publicly proud of the good reputation of his apartment house. Around the corner he was running a whorehouse, stocked with a several runaway teenage girls. Very low-key and exclusive. The other pimps didn't know about it, much less the cops. The righteously indignant Owen Scully took bribes."

"Let me guess the priest's hypocrisy," I said. "He's a pedophile."

"Trite and not true. No, this old phony lost his faith twenty years ago but was too afraid of having to earn his living in the outside world. He's a devout atheist." The priest smiled. It was a beatific expression reminiscent of Barry Fitzgerald movies.

I felt like a fishwife gathering facts about a particularly grisly accident. I could not stop asking questions. I wanted to know why each of its victims had behave so bizarrely on the nights just preceding their deaths.

"I suppose I should be satisfied just reveling in their memories, in the sheer joy of human intellect. But once I'm wrapped around their brains, I can't resist the rush of chemicals that flow through me when I suppress these people's inhibitions and let them do exactly what they long to do. Tank wanted to feel just once what it would be like to be a woman. LaTrina hadn't acted the grand lady outside the country in almost a year. Eddie was tired of hearing good music second hand. Owen Scully had always wanted to kill. This coot wants to piss in the sacramental wine and let the other priests drink it. So, am I the monster…or are they? Am I doing good or bad in killing them?"

"That's not for me to judge," I said. "You can tell all this to the authorities and let them decide."

"There may be nothing left to question if you don't let the priest's legs down," it answered, in a laboring tone. "He's not a young man, and his feet and hands have gone dead already. Now he's having trouble breathing. You may be the one killing him."

Warily, I rolled the priest onto his stomach. Then I loosened the belt that held his feet up against his buttocks. The instant I did, he kicked back, catching me squarely in the groin. For a moment, my eyes were filled with a red as bright as Japan's Rising Sun. Then I collapsed to the ground, all my neural circuits overloaded with pain. I watched helplessly as the krypton light showed the priest bucking and shimmying like a wind-up toy whose spring had popped. A shrill scream of agony erupted from his mouth.

I regained enough control to roll away from the writhing man. In another few seconds I was finally able to gasp in a ragged breath. While I filled my lungs, I watched a projectile hemorrhage of blood explode from the priest's nose and mouth. Suddenly, he lay still. Out of his mouth, like a stream of nothingness, flowed the thing that had invaded him.

The adrenaline of fear brought me to my feet. I watched in horror as the being became a long shadow, roughly mimicking the shape of the dead man. It was so thin that it conformed to the blades of grass over which it flowed. Yet in the powerful light I could just make out a network of hair-width nerves running beneath its surface.

It glided in my direction. I fire the revolver at it until all the chambers were empty. It seemed totally unfazed. The holes closed up within seconds. I snatched the flashlight from the ground and thrust it forward. This, at least, bothered it. It shrank back. I focused on its center. It retreated, picking up speed. I was amazed by its noiseless quickness. I realized that it was trying to flank me and attack from behind. I pivoted the light around, driving it back. With much effort and movement, I herded it toward the edge of the park. The only thing I could think of was to force it into a busy street, where heavy vehicle tires could mash it so flat that it couldn't survive. I did not see the storm drain soon enough. By the time I realized it was there, the thing had half vanished down it. And then it was completely gone.

My father – may he rot in Hell – fancied himself a great wit. One of his favorite jokes was about Queen Elizabeth II and Prince Philip, Duke of Edinburgh. On their wedding night the Queen said, "Sir I offer you my honor." To which the Duke replied, "Madam, I honor your offer." And the rest of the night it was honor and offer, on her and off her.

Not content to leave this a disembodied play on words, when I and my fraternal twin sister were born, dear old "Da" insisted that we be named Siobhan and Siobhough. Shove on and shove off. The joke was on him. We've been shoving together, literally inseparable, since age fifteen. No fools, we knew that sooner or later we'd be caught in the great crime. Caught and permanently separated. They only way to stay together was to flee to another country and take up new identities, as husband and wife.

I telephoned what I had learned in Tobey Park to an expectedly incredulous Detective DePiano. I made the call from Nashville. There was no way we were hanging around in Memphis. Siobhan and I lived close to where a storm drain empties into the Wolf River. I doubt that the smell of hypocrisy would be stronger on any other residents of Memphis. We won't be back there again until we know for sure that it's been destroyed. Never mind Friday morning confession. If your heart's not as pure as the driven snow at the North Pole, I suggest you stay out of that fair city as well.

Sleigh Bells Ring
(From *Horrorzine* as *In a Winter Wonderland*)

Bruno Cavaliero pressed the power button on the La-Z-Boy recliner and sighed at the comfort of its plush padding and "baby's-ass-soft" leather.

"Angie, throw another couple logs on the fire," the boss directed. While his right-hand man set down the instrument that swept rooms for bugs and rushed to do his bidding, Bruno looked around and told himself yet again how smart he had been in buying the Catskill vacation home three years earlier. He had only used the place six times since purchasing it with the profits from the insurance payoff on Dan Travis, but it was more than a retreat from the Bronx; it was an investment for sale when he eventually retired to Reno, and it was an isolated venue for the annual "Keep the Peace" meeting with the two other branches within the Genero syndicate.

The shape of the snow-covered house reminded Bruno of the white headpiece worn by Sally Fields in *The Flying Nun*, a TV show his mother watched religiously during his youth. The central area was a huge A frame, with large wings on either side. The six bedrooms could accommodate the top men of the borough's garbage collection cum road construction cum business protection cum betting outlets cum pawn shops cum drugs cum money laundering cum loan sharking operations. Moreover, there were only three chalets – each surrounded by twenty acres – on the looping road that topped a half-mile dirt lane running through fir trees from Kelly Bridge Road. The other two properties bordered Swan Lake, which was one of dozens of such remote and isolated bodies of water created by the glacial earth scouring of the last ice age. Bruno would have preferred one of the lake views, but the feature that had "sealed the deal," as he said, was that there was no possibility for any FBI or IRS agents spying on him or his cronies from the water or the land while they were in this particular house. Especially on a manifestly inhospitable day like December 27th.

Once business was concluded and everyone pretended to be of good cheer and totally content with the division of the Bronx among them, there would be snowmobile riding and the obligatory brutal snowball fight, followed directly by gunplay on the back acres: everyone showing his deadly skills to the others by shooting beer or wine bottles and empty food tins, and by exploding with great concussion and flames several portable camping grill propane tanks. As night descended, they would eat, drink and play cards into the wee hours, chatting about victims they had screwed over or murdered, raps they had beaten and who had which police captains and judges in their pockets. Then, around noon the next day, they would climb into their behemoth SUVs and head home to gather up their families and head to Caribbean haunts.

"It's starting to come down like a sonofabitch," Angelo Mozzani informed his boss about the snowfall. "I hope they don't turn around."

Bruno checked his Rolex and confirmed that the time was half past one in the afternoon. "Whaddaya think? They'll come all the way up 17 and turn round at the last minute? Working out our differences just before the New Year is critical. Things are tough enough from the outside without us keeping our own peace."

"They'll be here," declared Dominick Russo. Russo was Cavaliero's chief financial officer, in charge of both sets of books and money arrangements not set down on any paper or in any computer. Protocol dictated that the guests – mob boss Carmine Pintanelli and family capo Salvatore Genero – bring only one bodyguard and their respective CFOs. Among the complete list were six "made men" (although Angie and Gianni "Johnny" Ferro, Pintanelli's enforcer, had not done a "job" in four years). The other guests were Rinaldo "Skinny Ronny" Baptista, Eduardo "Eddy" Rivarosso, and Enrico "Muscles" Alito, who everyone joked was the life-size model for Michelangelo's David.

"We never been up here in the middle of a snowstorm," Russo worried out loud.

"Angelo's got the name and number of that snowplow operator in Liberty," Bruno said, "so shut the fuck up and make me some hot cocoa."

"Genero's here," Angie reported from one of the chalet's front windows.

"Get the machina d'espresso going, too," Bruno directed.

The business bones of contention were concluded within two hours, just as dusk settled in around the chalet. The others watched Angie's and Muscle's macho antics as they used the chalet's pair of Ski-doos, two brooms and two garbage can lids to joust. Bruno won the shooting contest for the second year in a row. After the blanket of swirling flakes and darkness shrank their visions to the limits of their headlights and flashlights, the group retired to the formal dining table. Bruno had had his wife, Gilda, order and pick up an Italian catered banquet that needed little further preparation. As the men dined in a desultory manner and drank liberally, they debated the merits of *The Godfather* trilogy against that of *The Sopranos* while they played poker, all wishing their lives carried more of the glamour depicted on the big and little screens.

At 10:00, the group gathered around Cavaliero's 60" vacation HDTV and found an early news program. The lead-off item was the stalling of an Arctic vortex over New York State, with a total of eighteen inches of snow expected by early morning.

"Marone!" Sal exclaimed. "I better not miss my evenin' flight to San Juan tomorrow. You shoulda bought something closer to the City but still with a lot of land around it, Bruno. Insteada this bad news, we could be watchin' some fuckin' Feds freezin' their asses off inside their cars."

Bruno looked out the back-porch windows with dismay. The thick, cartwheeling mist of snowflakes was accumulating quickly.

"Hey, Angie," he said. "I want you should call that plow guy right now and tell him to drive his truck up here at nine a.m. sharp."

"Okay. No problem."

Bruno half listened to the call as he and his peers watched a serious-faced anchorman reporting on the rest of the world's mayhem.

"He said no later than ten," Angie reported.

"Yeah, well you call him back and –"

Bruno paused as the TV and the house lights went dead.

"Holy Gesu, now what?" Sal exhaled with anger. "Wires down already?"

A few seconds later, power was restored.

"Not to worry," Bruno assured. "This place has a propane-powered automatic generator in the shed out back. It'll be like toast in here right up 'til we leave."

"Yeah, but no TV, no Internet, no landline phone," Carmine pointed out.

"We're roughing it. Just like our ancestors in Sicily a hundred years ago. Except with snow," Eduardo commented.

Bruno ignored the observation. "Use your cell phone and call that plow guy again, Ang. Tell him *nine a.m.* if he knows what's good for him." He ambled to the built-in cabinet that housed the entertainment electronics and selected a seasonal CD to brighten up the mood. The first selection was an instrumental version of "Walking in a Winter Wonderland."

"I only get static," Angie reported.

The rest tried their cell phones, to equally vain results.

"Another reason not to buy a place out in Nowheresville," Sal said acerbically. "The heavy snow must be interferin' with whatever tower serves the area."

Carmine Pintanelli dug into his trouser pocket for his keys. "My Escalade is the heaviest. Johnny, see if you can make it into that little one-horse town. Tell somebody in charge that the power lines and the phone lines are out up here."

"You got it boss."

Ferro pulled his outerwear from the hall closet, yanked it on, then used his feet and shins to plow out of the house and to the large vehicle. It roared to life. The headlights pierced the writhing white curtain of flakes no farther than thirty feet. For several moments, the wheels spun. Then the bodyguard eased up on the pedal, and the Escalade disappeared into the storm.

Bruno locked the front doors and turned to the gathering. "I never told you how I got this place, Sal," he said.

"Illegally, no doubt," the capo returned.

Bruno and the others laughed.

"Through Dan Travis," Bruno said.

"The ex-king of asphalt?" Carmine broke in. "Let me guess. You broke his ass, but it was his fault."

"True. Stupidity is a fault," Bruno said. "Travis's dues were three-and-a-half percent, same as all the other construction companies. But I originally quoted him four percent and said I'd shave the half percent if he did me one small favor. Said I'd be taking out a million-dollar insurance policy on his life and using it for laundering purposes. I showed him how we would pay in monthly on his behalf and eventually borrow against the policy. I showed him the statute book that states how the law protects the identity of those involved. He went for it. But the business we were throwing his way, the labor problems we solved...weren't enough. He was undercutting us on the percentage side. He frequented Nino's Pizzeria on Coney Island Avenue whenever his crew was doing roadwork out there. The coroner's report said the dynamite only knocked him out, but he died from the smoke."

"That was you?" Dom Russo said. "Christ, that killed three people. Fucked up half a dozen others."

"Yeah, but the Russian mob took the heat, which benefitted every one of the families. And I converted the payoff on the policy into this lovely piece of real estate."

"What was that...three years ago?" Sal asked.

"A little more," Bruno replied.

Sal shook his head and finished off his Jim Beam. "You shoulda warned me you were doin' it. At least you shoulda told that story three years ago, when we first met up here. What if me or Carmine had used the same laundering game on somebody else?"

"Yeah, you're right," Bruno said, the extent of his apology. "Mea culpa. Let's get back to the poker; I'm down fifteen hundred."

Forty minutes passed without further incident. As a bit of whimsy, Angelo had brought along a pair of wreaths with large red bows for the chalet's front doors. Under each wreath hung a ribbon bedecked with half a dozen sleigh bells. They had jingled merrily each time the doors were opened. At 10:58, they rang once more. With no one else expected at the house, with darkness enclosing it, and with the property's considerable isolation, every man inside the house started at the clamor. The three bodyguards reached reflexively for the pistols in their holsters.

"Johnny must be back," Sal Genero said.

"Yeah. I locked the doors." As Bruno moved across the foyer, he noticed through the long, leaded-glass windows flanking the doors flickering lights in the distance. He realized they came from the direction one of the other vacation homes, at the edge of the lake.

The sleigh bells sounded again, this time jangling insistently.

Bruno pulled open one of the doors. His eyes widened as he took in the images of two teenage girls, dressed in parkas, wearing knit caps and gloves, their legs in tights and feet in boots. Their faces were drawn into masks of fear. The younger one's eyes were red. Half-frozen tears defied gravity on red cheeks. In spite of the distress that contorted their faces, Bruno noted that both were beautiful.

"Help!" the taller and older looking of the girls cried. "Please help us!"

"Come in," Bruno invited. "What's wrong?"

The younger of the pair now burst into full sobs, struggling to catch her breath in between. Both rushed past Bruno into the foyer. The older pointed at the still-open door.

"They killed our mother and father!"

The rest of the syndicate came to their feet.

"Who did?" Bruno demanded.

"Three men. They knocked on our front door…and…" The older one was caught for a moment in her own sobs. "…when my father answered, they pushed inside and shot him and our mother." Her gloved fingers dug into the sides of her head, as if trying to squeeze the horrible sight from her memory.

"We were upstairs," the younger one managed to get out. "We grabbed some clothes and ran out the back way."

"Did you recognize these men?" Salvatore asked as he walked slowly toward the pair.

"We only heard them…three voices," the older said. "As we were leaving, I heard one of them say, 'We got the wrong house!'"

Bruno shut the doors and locked them. He stared silently at the other members of his syndicate.

"Of course we'll help you," Bruno said to the two young women, in as soothing a tone as he could manage. He pointed to a pair of straight-back wooden chairs that faced each other from opposite sides of the foyer. "Just sit there for a moment while I speak with my friends."

"I'm pretty sure they came from the house up the road from us," the older girl reported.

"What's your name?" Bruno asked.

"I'm Roberta. This is my sister, Gigi."

"How are you sure, Roberta?"

"We know the people who own that house. The Buchanans. They don't come up here until New Year's. We saw a silver Yukon Denali parked in front. The Buchanans have a green Ford Edge."

Gigi glanced through one of the front windows and screamed. "It's on fire! They set our house on fire!"

"You hafta stay calm," Bruno counseled. "It's the only way we can help you. Do you understand?"

Gigi nodded.

"Take off your coats and caps while I speak with my buddies, okay?"

Without waiting for their response, Bruno took long strides toward the other men. When he was close enough to speak under his breath, he said, "'Wrong house' can only mean one thing: One of the other families wants to take all of us out at once."

"Or the Russians you gave so much trouble to," Sal said archly.

"How did they learn about this place?" Ronny Baptista demanded hotly.

"Does that really matter now, jackass?" Bruno shot back. "There's only one other house left in the area. Either they set that fire to cover up those murders, or else they're trying to draw us down there. They probably don't know that these two girls escaped."

"So, what do we do?" Dom Russo asked.

Before anyone could reply, Muscles Alito gave out an attention-getting sound and followed it with, "It's only been snowing. Ice is what brings down wires. I'll bet they took out the power, telephone and cable lines."

"Which means," Bruno said, "that by the time Johnny was driving up to Liberty, they were already going back to the girls' house. He must be safe."

"But useless to us," Sal said. "I don't know how they can assume we'll see the fire if we're all in the back of Bruno's place here. Even if we did but didn't investigate, they have to figure we smelled a rat. Which means, sooner or later, they'll be up here to correct their mistake."

"Not if we take the initiative," Dom Russo said.

Sal smirked. "Said the pencil pusher."

"Hey," Russo returned sharply. "If it means my life, I'm ready to blast them. What do you think I carry a fucking gun for?"

"To show what a big, bad hoodlum you are," Sal said. He softened the remark by smiling and pinching the finance man's cheek.

"I say we take the fight to them," Pintanelli said.

Bruno looked to the girl-women sitting on the chairs, now free from their parkas and knit caps. "Let me get more out of these kids."

"They don't look like kids to me," Skinny Ronny declared, his eyes narrowed and the corner of his mouth turned into a lecherous smile.

Bruno said nothing, but he agreed wholeheartedly. As he returned to them, Roberta and Gigi stood. They both wore figure-hugging sweaters that revealed their shapely breasts. The older one was better endowed. Bruno judged that her bra size was already a C. Their knit pants were likewise skintight, displaying well-turned legs and taut, round rear ends. Both were poised on the threshold of full-blown womanhood. As if that were not enough, their faces were exquisite, with flawless skin, full lips, high cheekbones, huge blue eyes and shiny blond hair that the older had cut in a Flapper style and the younger had allowed to grow down to her shoulder blades.

"How old are you two?" Bruno asked.

"I'm eighteen, and Gigi is sixteen," Roberta answered.

"How terrible for you this is," he commiserated, even as he calculated how excellent they would feel lying naked under him. He determined that it would happen before the night was done. He had the benzos to drug them into a deep twilight. Then, once he and everyone else among his cronies had finished using them, they would both have to be killed and moved down to one of the other two chalets. They already knew a great deal, and within another hour…when the three hit men were dead…would know too much. "Are you certain those men didn't see you escape?"

"Nobody followed us," Gigi said. "When we got outside, we ran to the dark side of the house, where there are no windows."

"It's very dark there," Roberta added. She seemed to have regained her composure better than her sister. "Also, there are a thick bunch of fir trees only a couple yards from the house, so we ran in there. We took the long way up here. Every time we looked back, nobody had come outside."

"Good," Bruno said. "Listen: These other men and I are all FBI…undercover out of New York City. We learned that large shipments of cocaine are being smuggled into Canada through the back roads here. Those men obviously figured out we're here and decided to try to kill us. They just busted into the wrong house."

"My God!" Gigi exclaimed.

"We can't just sit here and wait for them to attack us," Bruno went on.

"We could help!" Roberta said with energy. "We know the Buchanans' house very well. They have a basement and a side door that goes down to it. There's a key hidden outside."

Bruno said, "That's good! You two should stay here and try to hold yourselves together. I can make you cocoa, and –"

"No, we'd need to come with you," Roberta insisted. "You'd never find the hiding place under all this snow."

Bruno looked at Salvatore. The capo's lids lowered ever so slightly, but Cavaliero knew precisely what the expression meant. The two girls should be disposed of as far away from Bruno's chalet as possible. Bruno took a long, disappointed survey of the two innocents' bodies, then nodded at his boss.

The decision was made to send Muscles and Angie down to the lake area, along with the three CFOs as back-up. Bruno and Sal would guard the house, and Carmine would hustle down the dark private lane as far as he could, to make sure Gianni had not gotten stuck. The six departed, with the girls leading the way toward the flaming house.

As Bruno dimmed the living room lights almost to black, he focused on the CD. Nat King Cole sang Mel Tormé's "Christmas Song." He watched the front of the house while Sal surveyed the back, both with Glock pistols in their hands. The snow fell heavily, with the wind blowing strongly enough to make the flakes fly at a forty-five-degree angle.

"Can't go to San Juan now," Sal said. "What the fuck happened?"

"I don't know," Bruno returned. "I guess we should have concentrated on a Peace on Earth meeting with people outside our circle instead. You think it's the Russians?"

"Could be. They're really taking advantage of the Land of Opportunity. Brooklyn, Philadelphia."

"They don't have the legal system in their pocket like we do. I'll get a boatload of them deported back to Mother Russia."

"If…it's them," Bruno said.

Sal walked casually across the room, with his pistol leveled at Bruno's heart. "Or is this a set-up by my esteemed host?" he asked.

"Don't be absurd," Bruno said, trying to act as unconcerned as he could. Sal Genero had gotten to the head of the syndicate by trusting no one and by dealing swiftly with suspected disloyalty with bullets or ice picks in the base of the skull.

Through the wind and across the many acres, Bruno thought he heard the faint sounds of multiple gunshots.

"Something's happening," Bruno reported. He opened one of the doors and peeked cautiously outside. More sharp cracks echoed in the distance.

"Bruno!"

The crime boss peered into the snow to his left. Carmine plunged forward, his mouth open, gasping for air. He had his gun in his bare hand.

"Johnny's dead!" Carmine shouted as he neared the two large SUVs.

Sal now stood on the chalet porch as well. "How?"

Carmine's teeth chattered lightly, both from the cold and fear. "A big fir tree was lying across the lane. That's what took out the wires. Johnny must have got out to look at it. Somebody shot him from behind. Emptied a whole clip into him. The tree had been chopped down. The car's front tires are flat."

Bruno looked at Sal. "That probably means four guys were sent up here. Those girls heard three, and that must have been at the same time as –"

"I got it," Sal said. "It could be like the Gunfight at the O.K. Corral down there."

Several bursts of gunfire echoed from the direction of the lake.

"Jesus!" said Carmine. He looked imploringly at Sal Genero. "What'll we do?"

As if to help inform the capo's response, the lakeside house that was not afire exploded as if it had been hit with a blockbuster bomb. The noise was tremendous, and even through the dense curtain of falling snow, a fireball like a nuclear bomb blast turned the isolated patch of Catskill land briefly to midday.

"God Almighty!" Carmine screamed. "What the fuck?"

"Somebody musta hit a really big propane tank," Bruno surmised. He looked at Salvatore. "Nothing to do now but see who survived."

"Even with all this snow, that could be heard for a couple miles," Sal said, after letting out a sigh. "Christ. I hate dealin' with small-town cops and state troopers. Even though we didn't do nothin'. My cojones are tinglin'; let's get inside."

The three mob men locked the doors and turned on the lights in both wings. Then they took up posts at various parts of the great room, watching for figures to emerge through the streaming snow. Robert Goulet sang "The Little Drummer Boy" with a children's choir. None of the watchers interrupted him. As the Mormon Tabernacle Choir began the "Hallelujah Chorus," Bruno rose from his chair.

"I see two lights coming this way from the lake," he reported. He pressed himself into the shadows near one of the windows that flanked the front doors. "Flashlights."

Carmine rose and approached warily. Sal continued to watch the landscape at the rear of the chalet.

"Those two girls," Bruno said.

Two ungloved hands rapped hard on the twin front doors. The sleigh bells rang out in counterpoint.

Bruno moved to the front doors and unlocked them. The sisters hurried inside. Their clothing and hair were covered with snow. They looked less panicked than they had the first time they entered.

"What happened?" Bruno asked.

Roberta, the older, said, "I found the key to the basement, and four of your friends went down."

"Who stayed outside?"

"A guy named Dominick," Gigi said.

"Great. They left the Shakiest Gun in the West outside," Sal lamented.

"We heard firing before the explosion. What was that?" Bruno asked.

"A few seconds after the shooting started inside the house, one guy tried to escape through the front door. He and Dominick started firing at each other," Roberta reported. "Dominick killed him."

"What about the explosion?" Sal wanted to know.

Gigi shrugged. "We were hiding back in the trees. It just happened."

"Where's Dominick?"

Gigi had a Justin Bieber book pack slung onto her back. As she slipped it off, she said, "He walked close to the house, looking at the guy he had killed. The explosion threw him backward. When we went to him, he had a sharp piece of wood through his chest."

Bruno could see that the capo's mind was working furiously on how to handle the aftermath of the bloodbath. Bruno, too, was assembling the pieces of evidence, but his mind was distracted, wondering if there was some way they could rape the young sisters and dispose of them before outside witnesses arrived.

"Where did you get that backpack from?" Carmine asked, pointing at it.

Gigi made a stereotypical teenage face, shrugged again, and said, "I was so scared by those men breaking into our house that I grabbed it without thinking when we ran away. I have a project due first thing when we go back to school."

Carmine glanced at Sal with a dubious expression. Sal reached for the revolver he had holstered behind his back.

A moment later, Sal tumbled to the floor. A dark hole between his eyes began to ooze blood. Carmine looked dumbfounded at the younger sister, who had pulled an automatic pistol from her coat pocket and fired at the crime boss. The pistol's smoke described a narrow line as she retrained the muzzle on Carmine and fired twice into his chest. He sprang backward, striking his skull sharply on the oak flooring. In spite of the immense pain filling his upper body, he groped for the revolver he had stuck into his belt. As his fingers tightened around the grip and guard, a hole appeared in his upper cheek. He lived long enough to hear the raucous report of the bullet that had created it.

Bruno had reached for his pistol the instant he saw Gigi's gun appear. At the same time, he registered from the corner of his eye the gun in Roberta's hand, rising toward his face.

"I lied about the backpack," Gigi told Bruno in an eerily calm voice.

"But, as you now know, we've been lying ever since we met you," Roberta chimed in. The CD had finished and begun again, once more playing "Winter Wonderland."

"Sleigh bells ring, are you listenin'?" Roberta sang softly. "We're the belles, come to slay all of you. If you don't want to die right away, take out the weapon with your left thumb and pinkie and drop it on the floor."

Bruno did as he was told. Time would be his only weapon. He had to hope that the fires and explosion had alerted somebody and that the police would arrive soon.

As Gigi took one of the high-backed wooden chairs from the foyer, Roberta turned the living room lighting up full. "Walk backward toward that open space. Slowly."

"There's no dead mommy or daddy," Bruno said.

"On the contrary. My daddy's been dead for more than three years. You killed Dan Travis in a pizza parlor."

From years of frequent lying, Bruno easily affected a look of complete confusion, followed by one of total innocence. "I have no idea –"

"My father told my mother about the insurance policy. He said if he ever met with an accident, even if it didn't seem to have been created on purpose, that you would be behind it."

"The pizza parlor that was bombed on Coney Island Avenue? That was done by the Russian mafia."

Roberta doffed her knit cap and parka. In spite of his abject fear, Bruno could not help reassuring himself just how beautiful she was.

"We choose to believe our father."

"And you and your kind need to be exterminated anyway," Gigi declared from behind. She had claimed her backpack and unzipped it. From it, she removed half a dozen industrial-size zip straps. She then positioned the straight-backed chair to face the chalet's kitchen. "Sit down!" Roberta commanded. While Gigi secured Bruno to the chair, Roberta said, "Our mother clued us in. My father shared everything with her. She was contacted by the insurance company, but she played dumb in order to keep us and herself safe. She thinks of Gigi and me as if we're still helpless little girls. She would never believe all the work we've done in the past three years to get to this night."

Bruno jerked his head back toward Sal's body. "I never did nothing that that man didn't tell me to do. And I never dared to not do it either. He was the one who ordered your father's death...for skimming profits, underpaying kickbacks. Your dad was no boy scout, ladies."

"Even if it were true, it's not enough to save you," Gigi said in a voice as emotionless as that of any hit man Bruno had ever known.

Bruno listened in vain for the sounds of sirens and possible salvation.

"You burned down two other chalets just to get to us," he stalled.

Roberta reached into the Justin Bieber backpack. "That was nothing. Hacking into your computer was the big challenge. I rented the Yukon Denali in your name this morning, with the information from one of your credit cards. We've left no fingerprints. The rest of the snowfall will cover our boot tracks. The final police report will be a bunch of question marks, but we're sure it will conclude that your three clans had a bad falling out. Or maybe another part of the Mob decided to bag you all...far away from The Big Apple."

From the backpack, Roberta pulled out a stick of dynamite with a generous length of fuse. She walked up to Cavaliero, bent, and unzipped his fly. Roughly, she stuffed the dynamite into the opening and partway down his left pant leg.

"We want you to go the way our father did," she said, patting his crotch familiarly. "But pardon us if we don't hang around to watch this last place go up. Thanks for the two Ski-doos. We'll take them to where we left our own car –"

"– and their removal will be the last unsolved piece of the puzzle," Gigi finished. She reached into the fireplace and, with the fire tongs, snatched out a piece of smoldering wood. "Got everything, sis?" she asked in a breezy tone.

"Absolutely. I hope you bought a million-dollar insurance policy for yourself," Roberta said to the mobster. She watched Gigi apply the pulsing-red, charred wood to the end of the fuse. As soon as it began to hiss and sputter like a Roman candle the pair moved into the foyer, behind Bruno's range of vision. In clear, pretty voices, the younger sister began singing, "Sleigh bells ring/Are ya listenin'?" Then the door slammed. Bruno stared at the noisy sparks of fire that measured out his last moments.

Bruno heard the twin snowmobile engines roar to life. He immediately thrust his body backward, causing the chair to topple. Once on his back, he wasted no time in tilting to one side and then onto his face, with his head and upper body lying over the remaining fuse. The flaming part of the fuse was just above his head. He struggled mightily to throw himself toward the crackling, sparkling fire, like a tuna on the deck of a fishing boat, seeking the salvation of the sea. He failed.

The flame caught his toupee and set it burning. Bruno screamed from the searing pain, inhaled the stink of his flesh. With a gargantuan heave made possible by the adrenaline of injury and panic, he managed to roll over a full turn.

The fire atop Bruno's head went out. He laughed aloud with the realization that he had managed to put out the fuse. He would live to rape and kill both sisters.

And then Bruno heard the fizzle of another dynamite fuse.

The last survivor of the post-Christmas massacre contorted his neck to look toward the foyer. Inside the front doors lay three banded dynamite sticks, with flickering fuses almost upon them.

"Bitches!" he yelled.

The Midnight Show
at the Pink Palace
(From *More Monsters From Memphis*)

John G. Saxe dragged his fingers along the length of new railing, then lifted them to his nostrils to test for the familiar tang of brass. No smell at all. A micro-thin layer of something synthetic coated the metal. It would take a few weeks of sweaty palms running along it to wear away the protection. That erosive process would begin in three days. The Memphis Pink Palace Museum had been under renovation for the past five years and was almost ready for the official reopening. Spic and span from stem to stern. A shining fun house for the educationally inquisitive. Much more now with the addition of the planetarium and the IMAX theater. Not to mention the totally unexpected addition that had fallen from the sky. Literally.

Saxe was director of the Sharpe Planetarium. He had been number two at The New York Museum of Natural History's Hayden Planetarium for six years and was bursting with proprietary pride at finally having a quarter-million-dollar, state-of-the-art celestial projector toy all to himself. He had turned down the offer of directing the planetarium at the State Museum of New Jersey two years earlier, merely because he was on the short list for the Sharpe. Why settle on the used sedan when the keys to the new sports car were being dangled in front of you?

The hour was fast approaching midnight. Middle of the workday for a man in the astronomy profession (if only in a reproductive capacity). Besides, even if the museum was not yet reopened, there were always people bustling through it during the daytime, making noise, demanding his attention, needing the lights on. He got so much more done at night. And he had a great deal more to do; far more than he or anyone else had anticipated with only three days until the official opening. Nevertheless, before turning to his labors, he decided to treat himself to the grand tour. Before tiny hand prints marred the walls and the buttons that made exhibits come to life were abused into non-functionality.

Saxe took his bow-tied, seersucker-suited, crepe-soled self into the old part of the museum. It was called the Pink Palace because of the blush-tinted stone that formed its exterior. It had originally been intended as the supermansion of the inventor of the supermarket, Clarence Saunders. His self-service Piggly-Wiggly markets were to the superstore what Ford's assembly line had been to the automobile industry.

Unfortunately, Saunders fell victim to another supermarket – the late-1920's New York Stock Exchange. He lost most of his fortune and was never able to move into the giant structure. In 1930 it had been donated to the city of Memphis and languished until someone hit on the idea of turning it into a museum.

The director strolled admiringly past the replica of the Piggly-Wiggly supermarket that displayed row after row of neatly stacked items;

through the sepia-toned retrospective on Old Memphis; past the diorama of a turn-of-the-century apothecary, with its mortar and pestles, its dark bottles filled with nostrums and snake oils and its "coke flats" of legal cocaine (for a quick "shot of pep"); by the hand-carved miniature circus with plenty of animation to delight the children; past the natural, mineral, and fossil exhibits and the full-scale replica of the dinosaur. Not The New York Museum of Natural History – but a success, nonetheless.

At the juncture of the old and new museum wings, Director Saxe came upon the night guard. Appropriate to all the other renovations, the young man was a replacement for the Methuselah who had held the position ever since Saxe had arrived from New York. Saxe was perpetually poor at retaining names, even though he counseled himself again and again to pay better attention when he was being introduced. This lapse promised to become increasingly embarrassing until he got the new guard's name fixed inside his head, since he was sure to see him night after night. It was the same as one of the early-twentieth-century presidents. Calvin. Or Woodrow. But not Warren or Theodore.

"Three more days, eh?" Saxe offered, still walking. His words echoed off the hard, high walls.

"Yep," CalvinorWoodrow returned. "Then this museum turns into a zoo." His smile was dazzling white against his ebony skin. "Makes me glad I'm on nights." His crisply pressed uniform and gold badge looked all business, even though he carried no gun, no handcuffs, not even a truncheon. Just a flashlight and a cellular phone. Saxe laughed lightly at the man's last words, to give the impression he considered them colleagues.

Director Saxe picked up his pace as he escaped the conversation, moving along the hall that dead-ended at the mouth of the planetarium. There, outside the large, circular room, dividing the hallway, sat his unexpected treasure. Eleven-thousand-eight-hundred-and-forty-three pounds of meteorite, freshly fallen from the cosmos. Fallen (actually two weeks earlier) along a trajectory shallow enough to preserve the central core intact but fast enough to create a new canyon hazard across the fifteenth and sixteenth holes of the Farmington Country Club and reduce one winsome foursome to a gruesome twosome. In spite of liberal watering, much of the back nine of the club had been reduced to ash. Three houses, two cars and a score of trees around the perimeter of the course were damaged or destroyed by chunks that had ripped off the main body. Another small forest of trees was sacrificed to print the newspapers describing the biggest rock star to hit Memphis since Elvis. It was a must-have for the Pink Palace Planetarium. Saxe abandoned all other activities the moment he learned about it and focused on the procurement and transport of the alien rock.

It took a day for the meteorite to cool off enough to be touched, another three days for Saxe to secure ownership. Two days to have a crane hoist it onto a flatbed truck. Five more to finish fashioning its pedestal. But now it was safely inside the museum. As soon as the director had purchased the space rock, he had reformulated the opening of the Sharpe Planetarium. His mind had not been mathematically keen enough to earn a degree in astronomy, but it possessed more than sufficient showmanship to bring the wonders of the heavens to the common man. John G. Saxe had prepared and advertised the planetarium's inaugural show to be "The Search for Extraterrestrial Life." But that extravaganza was now bumped behind "Cosmic Whispers" and "Autumn Nights." This gift from outer space was just too big not to capitalize on. Riding on the comet tails of the summer's two meteor disaster flicks, Saxe had cobbled together a cautionary light show tale he had entitled, "Doomsday from Heaven." Arnold Feldspar, his assistant, had suggested the subtitles, "Meteor Maker" and "Bad Day from Black Rock," but Saxe dismissed both puns as far too déclassé.

Big, black, at once smooth and rugged, the meteorite dominated the entrance to the planetarium. Saxe stood directly in front of it. From his venue, it looked like a huge cigar. Or the fecal matter of a seriously constipated Godzilla. Tapered at both ends. Saxe advanced and touched it. It was cool to the touch. He balled his hand into a fist and rapped on the thing's nose. It gave off a faintly metallic ring. Balanced two feet above the marble floor on its steel cradle, it was beautiful in its ugliness. Saxe moved on into the great domed chamber of the planetarium proper. Behind him, the subsonic pulses of the IMAX show reverberated down the hallway. "Search for the Great Sharks" it was called. Saxe's movie parallel,

David Stone, was at work fine tuning the six-channel sound system for opening day.

Saxe went to the console of the planetarium machine, inserted his key, worked through the warm-up, then punched in the first cue of his new "Doomsday from Heaven" program. One of the slide projectors threw the title onto the curving ceiling. Sixty blue lights in the "pocket alcove" encircling the base of the dome mimicked a twilight glow. Saxe adjusted, fiddled, tweaked. The blue bulbs faded on a dimmer, through a count of twenty seconds. The next sequence he had already programmed in as well: a clear, midnight sky over Memphis, with the correct azimuth and declension for this time of year. The great machine canted and twisted noiselessly in the center of the room. Individual stars, constellations, even the Milky Way appeared over the perfectly curved, inverted bowl of the ceiling with such precision that the observer was easily fooled into believing that this was the open sky. A titan among optical illusions. Saxe moved his index finger over the master button.

"Hey, Mr. Saxe!" CalvinorWoodrow called loudly from the hallway. Saxe sighed, quit his seat at the control console with an annoyed attitude, and shoved through the heavy planetarium doors.

At first, all Saxe saw was the beam of the flashlight. He followed it back to its source. The guard squatted about ten feet in front of the meteorite. His head was cocked at a curious angle, like Nipper the RCA dog.

"Something's leaking out of the meteor. Looks like radiator fluid."

It did, indeed. Viscous, bright green, oily looking. And it was flowing down with more speed than mere gravity should have imparted. As if it were being fired out of a Water Pik. The puddle of liquid was already three feet wide, and the spray kicked droplets several feet beyond. At least, Saxe noted, it was inert to marble. There was no steam or sign of chemical reaction.

"Move back a bit," Saxe cautioned. "It could be toxic. You keep watching it and I'll get a metal bucket. A worker left one in my office. I'll be right back."

This just keeps getting better and better, Saxe told himself, his excitement going nova. More press. A visit from NASA. Maybe a new compound from light-years distant. Named after him. He had to remind himself to keep his feet moving. When Saxe returned with the galvanized steel pail, the puddle had grown to a pool. He pulled up to a halt, well back from the meteorite.

"It stopped about a half minute ago," the guard reported. "Wait! Something else is coming down. It looks like…" He got onto both knees, put his head close to the floor, and played the light up from a low angle. "…like a string with…"

CalvinorWoodrow's sentence was terminated by a short, sharp "pop." An instant later the guard collapsed clumsily forward. He made no more noise. Only his flashlight sounded metallically as it struck the floor, louder even than the John Williams JAWS music emanating from the IMAX.

"Franklin?" Saxe called out (for the shock of the moment had suddenly jogged his memory). "What happened?"

The flashlight had remained on. It was throwing its beam at an angle out of the guard's right hand, across the pool of liquid into Saxe's line of sight, so that he had trouble seeing more than the guard's prone and immobile body. The light also caught what Franklin had guessed was a string. Down its length glided a tiny figure, inside what looked for all the world to be a golden space suit.

Saxe was struck speechless by the sight. Nor could he find the neural paths to command his legs to move. He watched frozen in place as the creature, less than three inches tall, released its grip on the silvery thread, spread its three legs like a tripod, reached into a bulge on its golden suit, withdrew something as big as a safety pin, and blew a dime-sized hole in the top of the guard's head. In the burst of golden light, Saxe was able to see that this was a second hole. The first was slightly above the bridge of Franklin's nose. Blood spurted from each nostril, to mingle with the iridescent green.

The director realized that the creature's organs of sight were on the top of its body, as the suit was crowned with a clear material. Little winking dots of light could be seen through it, like many eyes blinking. Its torso seemed octagonal, and two arms extended from opposite sides. It waded fearlessly through the green liquid, first the two outer legs in tandem, then the central leg advancing, heading straight for the guard's corpse. Down along the thread slid a second alien, this one clad in a silver suit.

Saxe's neural circuit breakers finally kicked in, and he backed away from the meteorite with silent steps. When responding to the guard's call he had opened one of the planetarium doors so hard that its base latch had locked in place. He retreated through the opening, into the domed room's shadows. His ears throbbed, telling him he needed to begin breathing soon if he didn't want to pass out.

The silvery thread was replaced by a tiny mechanized hoist. In quick succession, four more aliens joined the first two. The colors of each metallic suit were different. Now added to gold and silver were copper, iron rust, cobalt blue and cadmium yellow. As if on silent command, beams of light burst from each suit – powerful, narrow-focused torches. The aliens turned, their searchlight tracks sweeping back and forth, making the hallway look like the night sky over a Florida theme park.

John Saxe retreated farther into the planetarium, determined not to be caught in one of the beams and receive a hollowed-out skull due to absence of mind. He was quite fond of his brain and was using it furiously at the moment, admiring the little explorers' ingenuity. How clever to enter a planet that had an atmosphere inside the protection of a giant hunk of rock, to have it take the punishment of the friction of entry and to absorb the abuse of impact. In fact, with his new knowledge he realized that three raised lines of ferrous rock equidistant and parallel with each other on the trailing end of the meteor might have been fins before being ruined and made unrecognizable by atmosphere and impact. Perhaps, he thought, the green liquid was an inner shock absorber. Or maybe the fuel to return home.

If they intended to go home. Plans of conquest seemed absurd. If it weren't for their lethalness, their size would have made them comical. And how many of them could be crammed into an eight-foot-long rock anyway?

Unless they were the vanguard of a mass invasion. First the devastation of a million meteorites hitting Earth; then the havoc of six million alien combatants fanning out over the land masses. Saxe felt rivulets of sweat trickling down his face. What if the world's Collective Unconsciousness had been honing in on danger from Out There over the past couple decades, as proven by Hollywood's outer space mania? *Meteor*, *Armageddon*, *Deep Impact*, *Invasion from Mars*, *Alien*, *Independence Day*, *Species*, *Starship Troopers*, *Men in Black*. Maybe even *Toy Story* and *Small Soldiers* had been preternatural, subconscious outcries. Was this how The End began…in a hallway of the Pink Palace?

Saxe gulped and retreated another step. It could have been worse. Stephen Hawking was the celebrity scheduled to open the planetarium three days hence. What if the aliens had descended from the meteorite while he was delivering his synthesized benediction from his wheelchair? Talk about a sitting duck.

He could still see the six suited creatures in the throw of the guard's flashlight. They were moving off in pairs: gold with silver, iron with cobalt, cadmium with copper. The director backed two more steps, then pivoted and dashed for his office. He threw himself inside and locked the door. His first impulse was to call the police, the National

Guard, NASA and the Pentagon. His second impulse was to curse. Some glitch in the museum's PBX had rendered his telephone useless for the past two days. On the other hand, his computer was working perfectly and was hooked to a line independent of the PBX. He could activate his e-mail and send a 72-point message to everyone on his personal list. Surely someone would be at his or her computer somewhere in the world.

Saxe paused with his fingers curved over the keyboard. What the hell should he type? Little green men from Mars attacking. Strike that. No one would take him seriously, in spite of the fact that he was known to have no sense of humor. What about the details of "Little gold, silver, iron, cobalt, copper, cadmium space-suited creatures from Out There running amok in the museum"? Still too bizarre to be believed. Instead, he typed:

HELP! This is no joke. Armed robbers are inside the Memphis
Pink Palace Museum and have killed the guard. I am locked in
my office. Phone not working. Please send armed and cautious
law officers immediately.

After he had finished, Saxe put his ear to the door and listened. All he could hear were the sounds of the musical score to "Search for the Great Sharks." Evidently, Director Stone had left the IMAX theater's front doors open. Then he heard the distant crash. For all he knew, the Creatures from Beyond could be setting the whole museum afire. That would definitely not do. The emergency doors to the planetarium were still chained and padlocked shut from the inside. The only avenue of escape for Saxe was past the meteorite. He decided to make his move before the whole place went up in flames.

Saxe had no weapon to protect himself. He emptied into the pail the marbles that were inside his crystal vase, along with his glass paperweight Planets of the Solar System collection, every pen and pencil he could find, a dollar sixty-seven in change, and all the loose paper clips in his desk. He turned off the office light, stealthily unlocked the door and peeked outside.

It was damned dark in the planetarium, with only the light from the projector casting pinprick stars on the dome. Saxe relied on his ears as much as his eyes. He took a few tentative steps into the aisle. A mouse-like noise near the floor caused him to whirl in that direction. The pail jerked involuntarily upward in his hands.

A beam of golden light knifed up through the darkness, struck the pail and ricocheted off it, reflecting the deadly beam into one of the seats on the far side of the room, causing the seat's flame-retardant upholstery to smoke. Saxe tipped the pail and rained missiles down whence the beam had originated. An instant later he was running in the opposite direction, rounding the large circle of the planetarium at near-Olympic sprinter speed. His attacker had been about a third of the way into the chamber. As Saxe neared the open door from the opposite side, he saw nothing on the floor as far as his eyes could discern. He aimed himself for the opening, but as he hurtled through it, his left shoulder struck the unopened door such a powerful blow that it rammed into its floor lock and then also remained open. Saxe threw the pail down the right side of the hallway, hoping to distract any of the little bastards that might be lurking near the meteorite. It banged and clattered along the marble floor and into the wall as Saxe dashed, jinked and darted down the left side, jumping over the guard's body with ease.

As he neared the center of the museum, Saxe caught a glimpse of two of the action-figure-sized aliens coming in his direction. He screamed for all he was worth and increased his speed. Whether it was the noise he made or his erratic onrush he never learned, but the blue- and red-suited figures made equally mad, three-legged dashes for the walls, offering Saxe a wide berth down the center. He was amazed at how quickly such small creatures could move, especially given that they were clearly in space suits. Then it dawned on him that they had been moving with great speed when he first saw them. Traveling at least as fast on their scale as he had been, as if intent on their own escape.

Saxe reached the employee entrance, unlocked it and threw himself into the cool night air, not stopping until he was at the far edge of the lawn. About a minute later, David Stone came charging out of the door, arms flailing, legs churning, eyes huge and wild.

"Jesus Christ, what are those things," Stone demanded to know.

"What did you see?" Saxe asked.

Stone gulped in several fortifying breaths. "I was running my show and listening to the volume from various seats when, all of a sudden, this silver light strikes the screen. Drilled a hole in it. Then another hole. I thought some madman with a laser gun was vandalizing the place. Then I realized whoever was doing it was shooting at the sharks on the screen. I had the sound cranked up pretty high, and at that moment it really blasted. I heard this high-pitched squeal that I knew wasn't on the track. I looked down over the rail and saw this tiny, silver thing dancing around in circles. It looked like a kid's toy robot, holding its hands up to a fishbowl helmet. Really well-made toy, I thought, because its movements were so articulated and balanced. I went down the steps. By the time I got to floor level, I saw it turning the corner toward your wing. Then I knew it wasn't a toy at all. What the hell is it?"

"A creature from inside the meteorite!" Saxe told Stone.

"Damn! I was afraid you'd say that. Well, I would have been out here sooner, except that when I came close to the intersection another one in a gold outfit comes galloping by at high speed. And it's shooting its little weapon behind it wildly, like it's covering its retreat."

"Where was it coming from?"

"The dinosaur exhibit."

Saxe's stomach convulsed involuntarily. Laughter escaped his lips.

"What's so damned funny?" Stone demanded.

They're frightened," Saxe replied. "Think about it: They expect to emerge from their rock in a desert, a forest, maybe halfway up a mountain. Instead, they find themselves inside a giant building. The museum's on a grand scale for creatures our size. Imagine how big it must look to someone two-and-a-half inches tall. One comes upon a seventy-foot-long shark swimming at him accompanied by screaming music. Another turns a corner and is confronted by a thirty-foot-high dinosaur. They were all beating it back to their rock to compare notes and retrench."

"Maybe," Stone granted, after a moment of consideration, all the while staring at the semi-lit and ominously quiet museum.

From behind the man, two police cars converged with "bubble-gum-machine" lights throwing red, white and blue light out in frantic spirals. The vehicles screeched to a halt close to Saxe and Stone, and four of Memphis's finest tumbled out, weapons drawn.

"You two on the staff here?" the cop holding the pump shotgun called out.

"We are," Saxe answered. "I'm John Saxe. I sent a distress call by e-mail."

"Right. We got two phone calls because of it. So, what's the story?"

Saxe glanced at the museum. "You wouldn't believe it, except that we have the proof." He launched into a New-York-City-speed synopsis of what had happened. When he came to the moment when he had deflected the death beam with the galvanized bucket, a buzzing and hissing issued from the bowels of the museum, toward the planetarium end.

"You say they're less than three inches high?" the self-declared leader of the lawmen asked, working hard to believe what he had heard.

"Hey, don't let size make you cocky," Director Stone warned. "These things are deadly."

"Right. But we'd better see what we can do," the leader decided, "before this city property is completely destroyed." To his partner he said, "Howie, call in for reinforcements. SWAT level. And make sure they've got riot shields." Then he jogged toward the employee entrance door, which still stood ajar. The other two officers followed, with weapons drawn.

"You want to see what's going on?" Saxe asked Stone.

Stone shook his head. "I'll read about the rest in the paper."

Saxe took his time crossing the lawn, eager to let the police assess the danger first. He followed the echo of footsteps into the museum, leading toward the planetarium wing. When he turned the corner, he found the three cops fanned across the width of the hallway with their weapons raised, a respectful distance from the meteorite. Past them, a blinding light escaped the rock, all along a line that bisected its length. The buzzing and hissing was like that of a lumber mill and steel factory combined.

Before anyone could comment, the rock split in two, opening along its length like a clam shell. The light disappeared as both halves crashed onto the marble floor. The buzzing and hissing faded to silence. The cop with shotgun ventured two steps closer.

"Don't be a hero, Billie Lee!" one of the other cops cautioned. "Let's wait for some heavy backup."

"Yeah," the third cop chimed in with an awed voice. "Like a bazooka."

The silence was replaced by a hum which grew louder and more high-pitched by the second. It was like listening to a jet engine through a window fan. The meteorite began to shake. Saxe and the cops retreated around the safety of the corner. Just as Billie Lee put his back against the wall, tremendous twin concussions echoed down the hallway and shook the entire building.

"What was that?" the third cop whined.

"I think I know," John G. Saxe said. "They've seen enough, and now they're going home." He stepped back into the hallway, needing to know if he was right more than keeping himself safe. When he did, his cheeks elevated into a smile broad enough to draw the policemen out beside him.

On either side of the steel pedestal lay the longitudinally split "egg shell" of the meteorite. Each half looked like a rough canoe riding on the tortured river of the destroyed marble floor. Above the pedestal hovered an oval-shaped spaceship. It was about two feet high, three feet wide, and five feet long.

"Goddamned illegal aliens," Billie Lee said, fitting the shotgun butt to his shoulder. He squeezed the trigger and let fly a round of buckshot that pinged and panged off the silver shell of the ship but did no visible damage.

As Billie Lee ejected the spent shell, the ship began to move. Not toward the men but through the open doors of the planetarium and into its night sky darkness.

John began to laugh again.

"What's so friggin' funny?" Billie Lee demanded.

"The projector is showing the Memphis night sky. They think it's a clear escape route."

"Big ha-ha," Billie Lee returned. "And what happens when they find out it isn't?"

While Saxe was thinking about the question, the spaceship ignited its thrusters. Hellish flames roared down on the quarter-million-dollar instrument and the rows of seats circling it.

"My planetarium!" Saxe wailed.

The ship had risen to the top of the dome, out of view of the doors. All the men could see were the torrent of flames akin to those unleashed periodically at Cape Kennedy. The entire building quaked.

Billie Lee grabbed Saxe by the wrist and dragged him back toward the exit. "We gotta get outta here!" he screamed, over the roar of the alien engines. The other two cops needed no coaxing. Despite the distance they all were putting between themselves and the planetarium, the sounds did not lessen but rather increased in their fury.

John Saxe ran once more into the real Memphis night, re-crossing the lawn to stand once more beside Director Stone. He watched in horror as cracks appeared in the outer planetarium dome. He did not know how the noise or shaking could get much worse. And then, suddenly, the planetarium exploded. Blew apart like a nuclear power plant gone meltdown. A small piece of concrete struck Saxe before the main debris could hit him, driving him to the ground and saving his life. Stone, Billie Lee and two of the three remaining policemen were not so lucky. Neither were the patrol cars. Nor any of the cars parked in the lot. Nor a significant part of the formerly spic and span museum and the landscaping surrounding it.

When he woke up, two paramedics were gingerly placing John Saxe on a stretcher. Ambulances, police vehicles and fire engines filled the world around him, as did smoke and the hungry sound of flames.

"The cop over there is still ranting about an alien spaceship," one of the paramedics told the other. "I wonder what really happened."

"Probably a gas explosion," his partner opined. "This place was unlucky since the day it was built. My father calls it 'The Pink White Elephant.' Well, looks like nobody's gonna see the renovated elephant now."

Saxe offered no rebuttal. His eyes were fixed on one of the large signs advertising the opening: "Doomsday from Heaven."

The Fall of the Romanian Vampire
(From *WTF Books*)

Romania. If you're like most Americans, you only have a vague notion of where this mysterious nation is. If you thought "somewhere north of Turkey and south of Russia" or, better yet, "north of Bulgaria and south of Ukraine" you'd be right. But you have no idea why a country so far from Rome would have that name. The answer is that it was conquered and settled by Romans during the heyday of the Roman Empire, and while those descendants of Romulus were eventually pushed back from virtually everywhere else, a goodly number managed to hold on in the land between the Black Sea and the Carpathian Mountains. In fact, if you speak Italian and a smattering of Latin, as I do, you can actually navigate in Romania. For example, if you read the phrase "vizitati muzeul" you could correctly guess that it means "visit the museum." The public signs look just like the ones from the TV *Mission Impossible*.

Aside from this information the only other fact Americans know about Romania is "part of it is Transylvania, where all the vampires come from." Half right this time.

No, I'm not Romanian. I never was. My parents weren't. I live in New York. Within the shadows of the George Washington Bridge. I like all the shadows of my neighborhood, but not everything that slinks within them.

That covers "where." "When" is December 2011. The Heights is definitely not midtown Manhattan, either in the quality of living or shopping, but we do manage to fire up the holiday spirit. A good deal of that can be attributed to the current inhabitants: lots of Roman Catholics, more than half of whom were born in central America or the Caribbean islands. As everyone knows, those who have little chance of scaling the gringo class pyramid, those just immigrated from poor countries, tend to accept violence as part and parcel of day-to-day existence. So, we in The Heights have more than our share of violent deaths. During the first nine months of 2011, we had ten fatal shootings and seven fatal knifings.

But then the number went up. Not from shootings. Not even from knifings. The next six blade deaths were neck slashings. Severed carotid arteries. All made right to left; all of the same width. All the victims had been robbed of wallet or purse, and all had dressed in a relatively prosperous manner. The combined Special Investigation summary (dated December 4, 2011) of Precincts 33 and 34 speculated that the instrument was a straight razor, and that a left-handed killer had decided to make northwest Manhattan his happy hunting ground.

The New York Times and *The Wall Street Journal* – as national public records of social, international and cultural, and of business and financial news, respectively – could not give two shits about a lethal robber at the opposite end of their island. The TV and radio media, however, had just begun to focus their antennae on the welcome bad news. My interest predated theirs, because I happened to witness the predator's third takedown. Everything about it was wrong. At least for me it was very wrong. I tried in vain to get an answer for it for two solid days and then gave up and resigned myself to taking care of it on my own.

This meant preparations. It meant the kind of materials you didn't visit a local bodega or Rite Aid for and walk out with. But I took care of the logistical considerations. And in that time two more died.

Every day after that, as soon as twilight slid through the brick and stone canyons – which was about half past four as the winter solstice approached – I was out on the streets. I had taped a map of Upper Manhattan onto a piece of cardboard that had recently protected an HDTV and pushed a pin into each place where one of the bloodlettings had occurred. They described a roughly one-kilometer-wide circle around a locus of 133rd and Broadway. This was the ruse of a mind at least semi-intelligent, a plan to misdirect the police. I had watched him leave his third victim, noted well that his escape via a southbound bus would take him out of the circle. It made things difficult. I could not simply hunt the hunter. I had to take him down close to my place of residence.

The two-legged predator looked young, but that had no bearing on my strategy. The challenge was that he outweighed me by maybe forty pounds. So I armed myself with the biggest, baddest, bolt-of-lightning Taser I could order. I'm not talking about the hand-held variety you have to jam into your assailant's side and that generates 30,000 pants-pissing volts. I got the Taser X26 Civilian that listed for $999 ($875 by Internet) and is capable of penetrating a half-inch thickness of clothing with a pair of wires at fifteen feet, with 7.5M volts of shock therapy.

I dressed up like a mark and minced along the grimy sidewalks. My needs dictated my patrols, so that I felt like a character from *The Truman Show* patrolling a limited beat. Even though I confined myself to four square blocks, I was able to finish my admittedly restricted holiday shopping early.

At 9:15 on a Tuesday night I spotted him tailing me. It might have been the slight fake drag of my right foot or the two bulging shopping bags I was – as the true New Yorker says – schlepping. It might have been the carefully constructed slump of my shoulders. Whatever it was, my bait had worked. I rapidly calculated the route I must take, staying among the crowded sidewalk traffic until I was on the block of my apartment dwelling.

I paused on one corner while he pretended to be engaged by a poster kiosk opposite me. Finally, the sidewalk ahead was empty from the alleyway to the next corner. I resumed my slow walk. I knew without turning to look that he was crossing the street and timing his pace so that he would be beside me just as I came to the mouth of the alley.

I set down the smaller of my shopping bags, a festive holiday design from Bloomingdales, and shook my sleeve slightly, coaxing the Taser down into my hand. Then I bent, to make his attack all the more tempting. A moment later, I found myself propelled into the deep shadows, being bum rushed by an inhumanly strong creature whose clothes smelled to me of eastern Europe. The odor surprised me, but his power did not. I more than matched it by dropping to one knee, grabbing the lapel of his car coat with my left hand and aiming the X26 directly at the underside of his chin. Before he could react, I squeezed the trigger.

At point blank range, the double wires easily penetrated the skin stretched under his mandible bones, the same place a dog catcher jabs his pole hook when he is confronted with a dog suspected of having rabies.

I realized that the Taser had enough residual power to pierce the tip of his tongue and hook in the membrane covering his hard palate. For a moment, his cheeks lit up like a Chinese lantern. Then, accompanied by crackle and sizzle, he fell to the concrete and did a double-quick break dance. I eased off the trigger and scooped from my coat pocket two pairs of handcuffs. These were not the kind sold in adult toy shops or even to ordinary police departments. If Carl Denham had had King-Kong-sized cuffs made of this steel, the big monkey would never have escaped. I pushed his non-resisting wrists behind his back and snapped on both pairs. Then I went back for my second shopping bag, grabbed the first with the same hand, and dragged the killer none too gently halfway down the alley to the service door of my apartment building.

Where I live is old but in respectable shape. Four stories, with one service and one tenant elevator. Twelve addresses in all. What pleased me most was the dark back alley and a storage room in the basement that had a good deal of excess junk in it, which nobody seemed to want to access until they moved out. Among the items long ago propped against an inner wall, up on a skid and sealed in thick plastic, was a king-size mattress. I had augmented this with three others – one for each wall. To cover the ceiling, I had ordered anechoic foam, material extruded into rows of highly sound-absorbent cones. The stuff is god-awful expensive but essential.

Once I had the nuisance stowed inside my soundproofed room, I turned on the overhead light and gave him a good study. He was a handsome bastard, in a Slavic way. High, prominent cheekbones; thick, dark hair; cupid-bow lips. I could see why such an attractive man would want to hold back the aging process by a factor of a hundred to one. As he appeared at that moment, he could get women from eighteen all the way up to confident grandmother cougars.

Before he regained consciousness, I snipped away the probes and wires from his palate, tongue and chin. While chaining his middle to a column support that held up the building, I observed the amazing healing process of the vampire. The blood that poured out of his slightly open mouth stopped dribbling after twenty seconds. The two puncture marks under the curve of his chin closed within two minutes. By the time I finished securing industrial zip ties around his knees and ankles, his eyelids began to flutter. I noted that his irises had a distinct amber tint. When he ran his tongue over his blood-stained upper teeth, I observed the slightly overlong canines.

I slapped him several times across both cheeks. He focused hard on me, then tested the strength of his various bonds. It was at that point that he began to look truly frightened. I unbuttoned my coat and fished the crucifix out from the front of my shirt. I let it dangle inches from his amber eyes. His terror eased. He refocused on me.

"Nothing, huh?" I asked.

He remained silent.

"What about this holy water?" I asked, uncapping a tiny vial I had tucked into one of my pockets. I threw it at his mouth. He failed to flinch.

When I was refurbishing the storage area days earlier, I happened upon a half-length mirror. I fetched it and turned it toward the vampire. I bent and peered into the silvered image. It was reversed as it should have been, and displayed everything before it, including the face of the man turned monster.

He laughed at me.

"But you are a vampire," I asserted.

"Call me whatever you like," he replied.

I returned the mirror to its place of shelter. "What about Bela Lugosi?" I suggested, since his accent and even the timbre of his voice harkened back to the long-dead actor.

"How did you know what I am?" he asked.

"I watched you kill somebody about two weeks ago. You slashed her throat with a straight razor." Having said that, I dug into his left coat pocket, found the closed razor and claimed it for my own. "Then you put your mouth to her neck and sucked down about two pints of blood. Finally, you robbed her."

He shrugged. "I only pretend to be a vampire. I'm as human as you are," he professed. "There's a whole club of us in Greenwich Village, but all the rest drink tomato juice blood. Phonies and cowards, they are."

"I felt your strength," I returned. "I see your amber eyes. The extra length of your canines. You're the real thing."

He took a moment to digest my words. "What do you care?" he asked casually. "You're not a policeman, are you?"

"No."

"You're also not an honest citizen if you took all the trouble to drag me into this place instead of giving me to the police." He leaned forward as far as the chain would let him go. "My wallet is in my back pocket. You will find more than eight hundred dollars there."

"Not enough," I said.

"Then take the key from my front pocket. I'll give you the address of my apartment. You can go there right now. I have a box in my bedroom with more than three thousand dollars in it. That should be enough to buy your silence."

"You speak English well," I told him.

"Thank you."

"Considering you only came from Romania several weeks ago."

"You are guessing, but you are also correct."

"What made you move?"

"The new blood of the New World," he replied. He gave me an unhurried, assessing stare.

"I think I understand. You captured me because you also want to be a vampire. To have the joy of eternal youth. To have great strength and speed, and the ability to heal quickly if you are harmed."

"If that were so, could you make me into one of your kind?" I asked, leaning back against the mattress directly across from him.

"Of course, of course! You've seen in the cinema how it works. You cut my chest or arm and drink some of my blood." All the while he spoke, he nodded his reassurance. "What the writers and movie folk think is that you must die and then wake up cold and unbreathing. Undead. No, friend, I must let you drink my blood several times in one week. You will still live, but you will transform slowly. And you will know when that transformation is complete because you will develop a hunger for human blood. Touch my forehead. Am I cold as the concrete?"

I did not move.

"No, I am not. Have you not watched me breathing? Put your hand against my chest and feel the beating of my heart. This is much less sacrifice then you ever imagined, yes? But still you will no longer age or catch any disease." A twinkle of amusement suddenly lit his eyes. "And when you go to my apartment, you will not find a coffin filled with dirt from Transylvania. Like garlic, mirrors, crosses, holy water, being invited to enter a house, most of what you think is right is just nonsense. The inventions of ignorant peasants."

I continued to regard him without moving, even so much as blinking.

"What are you waiting for?" he asked. "What else do you want?"

"The truth," I answered. "It's the only thing I want." I pushed off from the mattress and went for a cardboard box. Inside it was a Sears DieHard battery. Brand new. Guaranteed for 72 months. I had already connected the jumper cables."

"What are you doing?" the vampire asked in a voice an octave higher than moments before. "What's the matter with you?"

Without reply, I connected the negative pole to the handcuffs and the positive one to his right ear. His screams made me very glad I had soundproofed the storage room so well. I let him burn for several seconds, then disconnected the positive cable.

"The street people you slaughter are just incidental," I told him. "Who were you sent to kill in New York?"

"What?" he gasped hoarsely.

"Who must you kill to earn your powder?"

The vampire drew in a quick, sharp breath. He turned his neck as far as it would go, so that he could regard me with eyes changed by sudden understanding.

I asked, "You weren't told that I was here, were you?"

"No, no," he managed.

"How many vampires does the devil allow to operate at any time?"

"Eighteen."

"Finally an honest answer. Six, six, and six. The true number of Lucifer. In what year were you born?"

"1980."

"A mere baby. No wonder you were so easy to catch."

"How old are you?" he asked.

"One hundred and seven. You were right; you're as human as I am." I reared back my upper lips and displayed my overlong canines. I followed up by removing my blue contact lenses and storing them in their case. I leaned forward to show him my amber eyes. "You also told the truth about not needing to die to become a vampire. Who did your demon tell you to kill for your monthly powder?"

"Two professors at Columbia," he supplied without hesitation. "The blind one I have already killed, pushing him down an elevator shaft. I was told to wait three months before killing the second, so there would be no ideas connecting the first to the second." He had been trying to break the handcuffs for the past minute and was only now realizing how totally helpless he was. "How long have you lived in New York?"

"Eighteen years."

"I don't understand," he said.

"I believe I do," I replied. I unclipped the negative cable from the handcuffs, but I did not bother to walk around to address him face to face.

"You are a brother," the young vampire cooed in what I guessed was his most ingratiating tone. "We are the same."

"Blood brothers, right?" I replied.

He offered me an earnest approximation of a laugh. "Exactly."

"What is the name of the demon you serve?"

"He calls himself Beroald."

"And through what image does he visit you?"

"I carry a figure of a mermaid carved from the bone of a whale. I purchased it in a museum in Bucaresti. What is your figure?"

"Mine is ivory. A netsuke of a Japanese shogun."

"What is a netsuke?"

I ignored his question. The youth of this era are ignorant beyond belief. "And who is Radu Negru?"

"Radu Negru? I think I have heard…Why is it important that I know this name?"

"Because you were chosen to replace him and apparently found very wanting in the balance. Professors at Columbia were the excuse, but you were sent to me. Once again, so that I could do the bidding of those powers confined in darkness and forbidden from the earth until Judgment Day. You were sent to be the executioner first…and then the executed. How ironic that you sold your soul to the Devil for eternal life and you won't even make it to forty."

Before the naive young vampire could fully understand my intent, I slapped a length of duct tape over his mouth. It truly is the solution for a thousand needs. The muffled screaming was terrible but not what I would call – in my expert opinion – blood curdling. I flipped open his straight razor and drew a deep cut into the nape of his neck. Not deep enough to bleed him out, but enough to allow me to drink deeply before his supernatural healing power sealed it shut. I was able to drink from him for three days before he died.

Three days after Bela Lugosi Jr.'s disposal, I was visited by my personal demon. It came just before I lay down to sleep.

"What do you have to report?" it asked in its voice filled with the smoke of fire and brimstone.

"Nothing out of the ordinary," I replied, turning the netsuke figurine so that the unmoving lips faced me. "Another huge Christmas tree in Rockefeller Center, a fresh crop of skaters –"

"Do not talk of the season!" it bellowed.

"Oh!" I exclaimed, as if finally understanding its question. "You mean the inept Transylvanian you sent here for me to kill."

"He is dead," the voice said, more declaration than question.

"No. I let him go," I lied. "Everyone deserves a second chance."

"Your powder will arrive late," it threatened.

"I figured as much. What with all those last-minute FedEx and UPS deliveries for…Hanukkah. But I have an extra three days' supply, thanks to drinking your failure's blood instead." The room lapsed into silence. I knew I had toyed with Hell as much as I dared. I sat on the bed. "Here's my version of what happened – and since you rarely give me the truth, I'll have to be satisfied with it. You were spoiled by Radu Negru. It's hard to replace a seven- or eight-hundred-year-old psychopathic, sadistic butcher, especially in these soft times. You tried to fetch water from the Transylvanian well once too often. 'Old ways are the best ways', right? But you were wrong. This one hunted in those ancient villages like he did here in The Heights. Befouling his nest there just like he did here. Of course, New Yorkers are far too sophisticated to suspect the work of a vampire. But not in the Old Country. They were visiting cemeteries with pitchforks and torches before you shipped him here. if my guess is right. You had to send him somewhere where English is the main language, since it's probably the only foreign language he spoke well. You sent him here to New Amsterdam on a quasi-bullshit assignment and knew I wouldn't allow him to live. Can't very well ask the normal humans to slay a vampire, but like they say in Romania, 'It takes one to slay one.' So, it was the dumpster out back for young Vlad Tepid, and you're now busy looking for someone much more clever. Someone more like modest, old me."

"The one you replaced was also smarter and more loyal than you," the spokesdemon from Hell replied. "Make no mistake: The Creator's faulty intelligent design continues to churn out frightening mistakes every day. Learn more respect, or one will come for you someday."

"I am contrite, sir reverence," I replied. And by that unrepentant response I knew that I was beginning to tire of the price I pay day after day for day after day.

"In the new year, you will move to Chicago," the voice said. "There is much to be done there, and far too many drained humans in New York."

"Happy New Year," I wished myself bitterly. I drained the last of Johnnie Walker and sank down onto the sheets for another tortured night.

From www.bloviatingzeppelin.net, July 2, 2012: "As the sun rose Sunday, New York City hit a remarkable milestone, recording just 193 murders in the first six months of the year. In that same span, more than 250 murders were recorded in Chicago – a city just one third as large…"

The Favorite Possession

I'M AN AD MAN. I'm the one who coined "There's no present like the time" for Breitling watches. I brainstormed the Vick's VapoRub commercial where Kenneth Branagh is coughing on a black TV screen. He turns on his skull-base lamp, revealing himself sitting up in bed in a Hamlet costume and says in his most plummy Shakespearean accent, "To sleep, perchance to dream." Then he opens his medicine cabinet, takes out the Vick's and says, "Ah! There's the rub." I've written a slew of ads that have increased clients' share of business significantly, thus steadily moving me to the top of my profession's food chain. This means I need to live relatively close to New York City, where most of the top agencies are headquartered.

My wife and I gave up on the unhealthy Chelsea district of Manhattan when our daughter, Caitlin, reached her fourth birthday. I was by then willing to work from my briefcase on the trips in and out of Gotham as the tradeoff for the fresh air open spaces, country club, public schools with high ratings, and lack of noise, grime and crime. In order to be able to live in suburbia, but still use the train instead of a car, the closest gentrified town south on the NJ Transit line is Metuchen, New Jersey. After three months of searching, we found a nice ranch house near the crest of Skytop Road. The online realty sites like Zillow and Trulia rated the place as worth thirty thousand more than the asking price. The sales rep confirmed the value, showing us comps in the Metuchen area. I'll give you her initials, so you can avoid her if you're shopping in that area: EKS. She's been selling houses for thirteen years. Her stated reason for the low asking price was because the previous family had needed to move unexpectedly to California and desperately needed the cash. I figured their move had to be unexpected; they had only lived on Skytop Road for six months. I should have known: If it's too good to be true, it is too good to be true.

The house had been listed for three days. We rushed to put down the good-faith deposit. Four weeks later, we were moving in.

Caitlin was given an important task: to see that the teddy bear she had had since she was a newborn arrived safely in her new bedroom. It had been a gift from my boss and was a quintessential Gund with black, shiny eyes and the softest "fur." It was by far Caitlin's favorite possession. She dragged it around most of the day and would not sleep without it. Consequently, the soft fur became discolored with the stains of dirty hands and dirty floors and matted from a thousand nights of being drooled on – what my wife Alice and I called "goobed." Ever the most literal of children, Caitlin had christened her prize companion "Brown Bear," just as she had "White Bunny" and "Pink Pony." I, however, by this time was calling the stuffed, slightly anthropomorphized creature "Thread Bear," because of its condition.

The first night in the "new house," I found myself being awakened by my daughter tugging on the sleeve of my pajama top.

"Something's making noise in my room," she whispered. Matter of factly. Not at all alarmed.

I shook the lead from my veins as best I could and allowed her to pull me into her bedroom. Sure enough, ever so faintly, but there nonetheless, came a sound like whimpering. Not crying. Muffled. Soft, but persistent.

"It's a baby," Caitlin declared.

"It sounds like a baby, but it can't be," I told her.

"No, it's a baby."

I had long since learned that reasoning with a child must be done very carefully. I chose the Socratic Method.

"Do you think the people who sold us the house left their baby behind?"

"Maybe."

"Why would they do that?"

"Maybe they didn't love it."

"But Mommy and I were told that the people who lived here before us are older than we are. Their children are twelve and fourteen years old. They had no baby."

"Maybe it's the baby of the people who owned the house before them," Caitlin said.

"But we've been all through this house today, Puddy. Did you see a baby?"

Caitlin smirked. "No. Maybe it's up in the attic."

"I was in the attic – three times – and it was completely empty until I put our holiday decorations up there." As I paused to take a deep breath, the noise came again. It did indeed sound like a baby. Not strong, but rather as if protesting pain in its sleep. "If a baby lived up in the attic, what would it eat?"

"Leftover Halloween and Christmas candy?" Caitlin guessed.

"Honey, the people moved long before they sold us the house. It's been empty for weeks and weeks. No one would be here to feed a baby."

"Then what is it?" my daughter reasonably asked.

"Maybe something just outside your window. Like a lost kitten. Or a mouse stuck in the air conditioning ducts."

"Or a baby," she pronounced. "Can we find out?"

I fetched a flashlight and a screwdriver. First, we checked her room's duct supply and return. We looked all through her closet. We even braved peeking under the bed. Then we moved outside and looked around. Nothing.

This went on for three nights, and by that time I was really creeped out. More than enough to share the situation with my sleep-like-the-dead wife. We began to imagine bizarre scenarios, such as a truly demented person planting a broadcast device and a tiny speaker in the walls. I removed the baseboards and the outlet covers. Nothing. We thought it might be a consequence of wind leaking through the window. I installed winterizing foam. Nothing. The sound seemed to come from nowhere and everywhere in the room. The entire structure rested on a slab, so that nothing could have been placed under the floor. I scoured the attic minutely. During all this, we labored to maintain merely mildly curious demeanors, so that

Caitlin would not become alarmed. For her part, she took it in stride. It was just something "my new room does." We bought a sound machine for her nonetheless, and gentle lapping of digital ocean waves (her choice among the machine's repertoire) pretty much covered the persistent, plaintive noises.

This was not enough for me. On the eighth day, I took off from work and marched into the realty agency and confronted EKS in her private office.

"Tell me about the child who died in our house," I said, after she had vomited the usual pleasantries through a mouth that looked like it had been Botoxed minutes before. She reacted as if I had slapped her. "Keeping in mind that you are just as responsible for full disclosure as the former owners and the building inspector."

"You think a child died in your house?" she dissembled, as soon as she could reapply her rictus smile.

"Well-maintained homes in this town don't sell for thirty thousand under value – not even if the family has to move quickly," I pushed. "Since the Taylors only lived in the place for six months, I figure it was the baby of the owners before that."

"It's just a noise," EKS said, more than suggesting she had engaged in collusion. "A noise that happens to sound like a baby. No ghost, no items moving around the house. It might as well be a squeaky back door."

"You can oil a back door," I argued, leaning in toward her. "I found nothing in the *Metuchen Criterion* or the *Brunswick Home News* morgues. My guess is an unwanted near- or full-term baby. Maybe born to Madilyn "Maddy" Miller. That was the name of the teenage girl of the next-but-last family. But no scandal reported in the newspapers. Nothing that my next-door neighbors the Whites and Timpsons were able – or willing – to tell me about."

EKS affixed her best empathetic face and shrugged. "Then probably nothing like what you suggest happened. At any rate, I can't get your money back with a concluded contract and especially across state lines."

I stood. "It would be difficult and costly," I agreed. "But if you don't want us to sue you for complicity, you'd better think hard about putting the house back on the market; finding a new, deaf owner; waiving your fees for that work; and finding us an normal home in Metuchen. I thought we had taken possession of the house. Instead, it's taken possession of us."

The size of her eyes told me she knew I meant business.

But then the situation changed.

Caitlin, the tiny trouper, had resolved to ignore the feeble sounds. We offered to relocate her to the third bedroom, but she was adamant about staying in the room with the view of the apple tree.

I, however, could not leave it alone. My bladder works like Old Faithful: about three-and-a-half hours after retiring each night, it wakes me up for emptying. Before returning to bed, I stealthily opened Caitlin's door and listened. The night after I confronted the real estate agent, the sound was gone. To be certain, I turned off the sound machine. The room was quiet as the proverbial tomb. I waited in the doorway, straining to detect the whimpering for a full fifteen minutes. I was ambivalently disappointed. The same on the next night and the night thereafter. I could not figure out what had caused the change. A begrudging, cautious optimism slowly lowered my defenses.

But the story was not done. One week to the day after the noises stopped, Caitlin made a matter-of-fact statement at the breakfast table. She had Thread Bear on her lap, with its usual calico napkin knotted around his scruffy neck. She had been eating a triangle of wheat toast spread with strawberry preserves and with the edges cut off. When it had disappeared completely into her mouth, been chewed with no haste and swallowed, she spoke.

"Brown Bear is breathing now. How did you make him do that, Daddy?"

I resisted the urge to snatch the stuffed companion from Caitlin's lap and instead first petted it, then lifted it slowly toward me. Nothing different. Just the same old Thread Bear.

"He's not breathing, Puddy," I said.

"Not now. Only in my bedroom."

Yet again, she showed no agitation. Nor should she have if she were simply using her imagination. But by this time, I knew better than to dismiss the statement as pure fancy.

That night, I glided into Caitlin's room and up to her bed. Her little arms were wrapped possessively around Thread Bear, and a slight smile curled the corner of her mouth. The window curtains were pulled back, and the light of a full moon were enough to show me that the bear's chest and tummy were indeed rising and falling with peaceful regularity. The baby had found a mommy.

So now, I ask you: What would you do? Finally, some dead, but not departed, child has obtained a degree of rest. My daughter is pleased to have her bear animated. But how far away is the day that she realizes such a thing is not natural? The Easter Bunny and Santa are exposed as benign hoaxes by the time most children are eight. One thing is true: We no longer need to move to another house. Not, at least, for the time being.

Where We Are

Bernard Schuster had been a bastard all his life. Charming, polite, urbane. But a conniving, self-centered, lying, cheating, thieving bastard. Succinctly put, Schuster was a shyster. Like Willie Sutton, who said, when asked why he robbed banks, "Because that's where the money is," Bernie realized by age fourteen that Wall Street was where the really big money is, and the robbers in control used guile rather than guns.

Bernie had formulated his antisocial philosophy of life because children are much more perceptive than adults give them credit for. The kids around young Schuster intuited that he was a conniving, self-centered, lying, cheating, thieving bastard. So, he found himself alone in all but situations where other children were forced to interact with him. He wholeheartedly ascribed to the old nursery song:

> There was a jolly miller once
> Lived on the river Dee;
> He worked and sang from morn till night,
> No lark more blithe than he.
> And this the burden of his song
> For ever used to be,
> "I care for nobody, no, not I,
> If nobody cares for me."

Bernie was a confidence man of the highest reaches. If awards were given out for the most audacious fraudulent returns investment schemes, Schuster would have won the 2006 Golden Ponzi.

Eighteen billion raked in; more than a quarter-million honest, if greedy, investors and institutions impoverished. Many individuals bilked at the end of their earning days, when any ability to regain financial stability was impossible. Bernie caused seventeen suicides and who knew how many heart attacks and strokes.

An interesting fact was that Bernie had lived fabulously well before hatching the believable bilk. The man had a penthouse on the Upper East Side and a fifteen-room beachfront "cottage" in the Hamptons. He had traveled the world with private guides. His succession of wives had shopped at Cartier, Lanvin, Akris and Oscar de la Renta. But Bernie wanted a yacht bigger than Hirair Hovnanian's mysteriously sunk Lady Anna. He wanted a mansion on Sunset Boulevard. He wanted to produce action films. He wanted to hobnob with movie stars.

Like all get-rich schemes, Bernie's eventually collapsed from a combined lack of new suckers and his voracious spending appetites. And so he went to the Federal Prison Camp in Yankton, South Dakota: A "Club Fed" that was once a college campus and which featured art lessons and a room filled with musical instruments. Life was still good, with HDTV, HBO, Netflix, a billiards table, extensive library and the best "imported" delicacies. His sentence was officially 20 years, which reduced to as few as 14 if he was a model inmate. The problem was that Bernie was 64 when he went away, and even then he was not in the best of health. Sedentary living and a 44-inch waistline had given him diabetes, asthma, hypertension and coronary heart disease.

In 2015, heart failure threatened to end it all. He needed a new pump. The U.S. government was obliged to keep him alive through his sentence, but they were not obliged to send him to the Cleveland or Mayo Clinics or New York-Presbyterian for a transplant. He would gladly have paid ten million from his hidden horde in the Cayman Islands to fly a top team and equipment into Yankton, but the moment he revealed the money the government would have seized it to repay his investors their pennies on the dollar. So, the screw turned on Bernie.

For two weeks, Bernie ate nothing but fruits, vegetables and nuts in a last-ditch effort to reverse the wages of wasting other people's substance in riotous living. When he failed to lose his target ten pounds, he gave up.

As the fateful medical day approached, he decided to consult the Torah, as W.C. Fields had done with the Bible on his deathbed, "…lookin' for loopholes." He regretted not having bribed his way into FCI Otisville in New York, the country club prison favored by observant Jews that had a full-time rabbi and an extensive religious program.

Throughout his life, the vast majority of Bernie's friends were atheists, believing, like Verdi's Iago, that after life, "And then? And then? Nothing." Bernie wasn't so sure. The contemplation of pure, unconscious annihilation didn't bother him – but an afterlife did. Because such a state might well betide the hell for sinners like him so feared by the Christians and Muslims.

By the time a heart was found for him, Bernie was resigned to having the procedure done by a South Dakota team. Several times a day, he prayed to a god he only half believed existed, a god he was sure was not particularly on his side, in spite of the spiels of religious men about His infinite forgiveness. Even as he intoned his words of contrition, he knew that in his figurative heart he did not regret a single act that had made his pre-prison life a heaven on earth.

But then, two days before his operation, Bernie happened to open a book penned by the notoriously amoral philosopher Niccoló Machiavelli. The Italian Renaissance advisor to Lorenzo "The Magnificent" Medici had written that he had no fear of Hell because, "In Hell I shall enjoy the company of popes, kings and princes, but in heaven there are only beggars, monks, hermits and apostles." If there was a hell, certainly it would be populated with the most interesting, colorful characters. With that thought buoying his spirits, Bernie found blissful rest.

It was on a cold Monday morning when Bernie was wheeled into the operating room. One of the other white-collar criminals at Yankton had assured him that Monday mornings were when surgeons were at their best. He was not (forgive the word) heartened. He would have preferred a pair of top surgeons on their worst day.

In spite of the warranty on his ticker being nearly up, it was lubbing and dubbing at 140 beats per minute before the sedatives kicked in. He smiled at the team who bustled around the operating table, but they returned impassive eyes above surgical masks.

"All right, Mr. Schuster, it's time," a nurse said. "Why don't you begin counting backward from one hundred?"

Bernie got to ninety one. Then unconsciousness set in. He had been under the knife during his life three times: to remove an inflamed appendix, to have four impacted wisdom teeth dug out and to scoop out the remains of a ruptured gall bladder and its contents. Each time, the ordeals were done as if in seconds. One second he was going under; the next he was awake. Not this time.

From out of the darkness came the most brilliant light Bernie had ever seen. A psychology journal he had read explained the phenomenon as a dying human brain reaching back to the first moments of consciousness, when the fetus emerged from the stygian womb into the delivery room's lamps. He waited with impatience to see if this was merely the rationalization of non-believers' minds or if the light of eternal life was opening to him.

He knew that legions of those who had had near-death experiences described shadowy figures appearing on either side of the light, as if souls already departed stood ready to greet their latest entrant. This was not the case with Bernie. Nor was there a heavenly gate, with a divine figure waiting to consult the Roll Book of Life and recite the verdict of eternal salvation or damnation.

When the light abated, Bernie found himself standing in a lush meadow filled with exquisite flowers. A cerulean blue river curved panoramically just ahead of him. The sky was an intense indigo, with puffy clouds floating by like sheep gently grazing. Somewhere nearby, from a copse of trees behind him, birds sang tunefully.

Bernie smiled. So there was something after human life. And it looked, smelled and sounded good. Really good.

He raised his gaze as he pivoted a full circle. He realized he stood in a verdant bowl, ringed on the opposite side of the river by a line of hills. The hills were lovely in their formation. Especially attractive was a mesa with high, vertical walls.

But the most exciting element of his vision was the figure of another human being. The figure stood so far away, at the top of the mesa, that he could not discern whether it belonged to a man or a woman.

Bernie waved. The figure waved back. Bernie determined to reach the other inhabitant of his new world. But the river was too wild and wide for him to wade or even swim across. He determined to walk along its bank until he could find a place to ford it. He walked and walked for what he thought must have been hours. The river raged on, impossible to cross. Whenever he looked up at the sun, it seemed to be directly overhead.

In spite of having the same body as he had arrived on the operating table in and spite of seemingly a full day of walking, Bernie did not feel tired. He trudged forward with fell determination. On his way, he had seen another far-off figure, standing at the apex of a monumentally tall tower. The figure had waved at him and he stopped to see if it would quit the tower and at least come to the opposite edge of the river, but the figure remained at the parapets, sweeping its hand back and forth, back and forth. Not lustily, as Bernie had waved, but in a slow, languid fashion.

Later in his day-lit journey, Bernie encountered yet another distant figure. This one stood on a viewing bridge, set in the middle of what looked to be a gigantic hedge maze. As the two other figures had done, it waved, but without apparent emotion. In all three cases, the figures were too far from Bernie to make out the expressions on their faces. He had tried each time to shout a "hello," even cupping his hands around his lips like a makeshift megaphone. But the separations were obviously too far and the tumbling river too noisy for human sounds to link.

On and on Bernie trudged, growing more peeved at the curving river's persistent depth and speed. He lowered his head, broke into a trot, and discovered to his delight that he did not grow winded. Through the knee-high grasses and flower stems he plunged, until he came upon a path that had been beaten down through the vegetation. The path was exactly the same as what he had been creating all day. He smiled at the evidence that someone else moved within reach of him. He redoubled his pace.

And then he happened to glance to his side. Across the river, under a sun that still blazed from its zenith, was the same mesa he had viewed so long ago. At the top of the mesa stood a figure. He could not be certain, but Bernie believed it was the same soul he had seen upon his arrival. It waved at him forlornly.

I'm on an island, Bernie thought with horror. An island I can't get off. Just as bad as being trapped atop a mesa. Or a tower. Or in a maze. This isn't heaven.

Alive, or in dying, or when dead, hell is where you are completely alone.

> Hell hath no limits, nor is circumscribed
> In one self place, but where we are is hell,
> And where hell is, there must we ever be.
> Christopher Marlowe, *Doctor Faustus*

Yantar (Amber)

An icy soul can prevent the most corpulent from becoming warm. Viktor Ivanovitch Protopopov was the character who taught me this truth.

According to my father, Protopopov had been large even when they were young together in the same Baltic seacoast village. Whenever a rude neighbor commented on his weight, he offered the same reply: "I hate being cold, tovarich, and I am always cold. I wear my extra weight like a coat, in the vain hope of ever feeling truly warm. The only time I am happy is when I eat, because the hot food warms my inner self."

Viktor and my father, Ilya Fedorovitch Khvorostinin, were approximately the same age. They grew up within a kilometer of each other. But they were never friends. As my father early realized, the rotund boy's cunning and avarice were engraved on his porcine face. His parents were hard bargainers but never cruel or callous. Why Viktor had evolved into such a creature no one could explain.

When my father was in his early twenties, he discovered an enormous layer of amber beneath the soil of the family farm. Soon, the entire village was digging for the precious fossilized tree resin that shone like a gem when broken and polished. To their dismay, the only other deposit of consequence was found under the Protopopov farm.

Baltic amber has been a precious commodity since before written history. I understand that it has been found in Greek and Mycenaean shaft graves from more than a thousand years before the birth of our Lord. Imperial Romans adorned themselves with amber buttons, necklaces, brooches and even had their seals carved into it to fashion signet rings. Patrician women used its ability to generate an attractive force when rubbed with a rough cloth in order to remove lint and animal hairs from their garments. Most prized were those pieces containing unclouded views of ancient insect corpses. To my family's great fortune, this passion had never gone out of fashion.

Because our village lay between the bellicose King Frederick of Prussia to our west and the equally militaristic Tsar Peter to the east, our Swedish liege across the dark Baltic was careful not to oppress and alienate us too sorely. The Protopopovs and the Khvorostinins both prospered. Our clan had more amber to sell, but we also sold it at a fairer price, so that the families grew more or less equally rich. We generally sold through middle merchants, my uncle and a hired neighbor traveling as far as England and Italy to sell directly to shops.

Then, in 1709, when I was but ten years old, my world changed. Tsar Peter and his allies defeated the Swedes at Poltava, and we were suddenly Russians. My father turned the focus of his trade to Moscow and Peter's newly rising city, St. Petersburg. Not to be outflanked, Viktor Protopopov followed suit. When, in 1712, Peter proclaimed St. Petersburg as his capital, the Russian aristocracy flocked to the banks of the Neva to build palaces and grand townhouses. More and more of both our families' time was spent there, accounting for about half our total sales. Even so, both families resisted relocating. Despite Peter's unflagging efforts to Westernize, the new city clung to its Tatar roots. What was worse, it lay significantly closer to the Arctic Circle than did our village, so that winter arrived a few weeks sooner and departed a few weeks later. Truth be known, my father disliked the cold almost as much as did Protopopov.

A second major event, however, compelled both families to relocate. In 1701, Frederick had commissioned the construction of the most splendid palace room ever to exist. Its walls were completely covered in exquisitely carved amber. It was installed in the Main Palace in Berlin, whence nobility from all over the world came in pilgrimage. In 1716, Frederick William I, successor to the Prussian throne, signed an alliance with Tsar Peter. In commemoration of the deed, Frederick William presented Peter with the Amber Room. The many panels were disassembled and shipped to the Winter Palace. When it was reassembled, ranks of Russian nobility flocked to gape at it.

Ever-popular amber suddenly became the rage of fashion. Our families redoubled excavation efforts to meet demand. We relocated to the ever-chilly, largely barbaric St. Petersburg in May; the Protopopovs followed in August. Old man Viktor's grumblings about being perpetually cold now became as frequent and vociferous as a Turkish muezzin's prayers. Although he used his stumpy legs only to waddle from chair to carriage or stool to couch, he did possess the discipline to rise early every morning and to work at his office until five o'clock, so greedy was he to earn ever more rubles and fearful that his clerks and salesmen might cheat him if they were not under his watchful eye. His daily habit was to grab a breakfast of steaming oatmeal and a lunch of scalding borscht, with a huge tea samovar by his side at the office, to keep the single glowing cinder of his black heart from extinguishing completely.

"Damn St. Petersburg!" Viktor would tell anyone who would listen. "My evening meal is the only joy left in my life." He made known that his townhouse had been chosen because the dining room had facing fireplaces.

My father catered personally to the Russian aristocracy. When I reached the age of majority, I took over the family trade with the Prussian, Hanseatic and Dutch states, as well as England. I learned the languages and filled the many hours riding in coaches by reading the great literature of those people. Numerous shops in the Netherlands had added quality pottery and porcelain, brought from China by the Dutch East India Company. I returned to St. Petersburg with samples of these wondrously wrought earthen treasures, both for my family's personal use and for sale. I found an eager market that, over time, contributed greater and greater percentages toward the family fortunes. The Russian nobility snapped up the delicate figurines and notion boxes but flatly rejected the utility of porcelain dishes. To dine on anything less than silver plates was to lower oneself to the level of the common rabble. The very few who could afford it indirectly signaled their lofty positions by dining on gold.

In 1721, Protopopov approached my father with a proposal of unions between our rival families. He wished to marry his only daughter, Raisa, to me. Ever since arriving in St. Petersburg, Viktor had been throwing money back at the lesser nobility, buying Raisa invitations to soirees and sleigh rides. At the same time, he hired a genealogist in a vain attempt to prove that his branch of the Protopopov tree had blue blood for sap. When none among the noble sons, poor or witless though they might be, would have the heifer, Viktor shifted his strategy in my direction.

"Her face is rather pretty," my father observed, after transmitting the marriage proposal to me.

"But the other seven-eighths is all fat," I countered. "And none of her weight is from brain matter."

My father smiled. "I have already taken the liberty of giving Viktor your answer."

Not a month after that, my father fell quickly sick, with a swelling of his neck and tongue that soon prevented him from speaking clearly. What power of communication he had, he wrote down, transferring minutely his years of amassed business knowledge. All too soon, the swelling threatened his breathing. I wondered aloud to him if he had not been poisoned by Protopopov at the last merchants guild meeting they had both attended. He shrugged at my suspicion.

And then, in early September, he was gone. I watched Protopopov carefully during the burial service for any sign of satisfaction, but all I saw in the old wolf's expressions were the same look of greedy cunning that had contorted his face since his youth.

I knew that I needed to stay in St. Petersburg to manage directly our business, but I also needed to transfer my trade routes to a trusted man and to accompany him once, to establish the many relationships I had nurtured. The fellow's name was Petrovski, a smart, witty and honest man. Together we rode, with four pack horses. Among our closest Russian noble customers were the exalted Naryshkins. Two of their young men, Nakita Melikov and Alexander Shafirov, learned that my trip would take me overland to our village for amber and thence to Konigsburg, where I would board a vessel bound for England. They, as well, traveled to Konigsburg, to study shipbuilding as part of Tsar Peter's continued plan to educate promising children of the aristocracy to Western science and technology. In imitation of Peter's penchant for traveling incognito, they wore peasant-style clothing. Beneath their coarse woolen coats, however, they carried the same pistols and cavalry swords as those that equipped Peter's crack Semenovski Guards. I welcomed their protection.

The four of us had ridden barely fifteen kilometers beyond St. Petersburg and just entered a dense fir forest when we were ambushed by three men. A light October snow covered the ground. I suppose to blend in with the pervading whiteness, each of the three attackers wore hooded robes of white. They appeared suddenly from behind the firs. Each aimed a flintlock. They all seemed to be concentrating on me, as one bullet passed so close to my face that the rending of the air tickled my nose. A second bullet pierced the sleeve of my coat without touching my flesh. Petrovski was not so lucky. The third bullet struck him in the neck, knocking him off his horse. I jumped down from my steed to drag him into the concealment of brush on the far side of the road. Meanwhile, my noble comrades charged directly at the brigands, shooting one between the shoulder blades and killing him instantly. The other two they hacked to pieces before they could reload.

Petrovski died in my arms within minutes. When I viewed the carnage my noble companions had wrought, I was astonished to see a face I recognized. It belonged to a man whose name I could not remember but who had labored in the back rooms of the Protopopov offices, cutting amber and fusing together small, inferior pieces with heat, to sell to the innocent uninformed. Clearly, if Protopopov could not marry his family to gain access to our clients, he would steal the business once I was murdered.

I shared this intelligence with Nakita and Alexei, who wanted to know how I intended to take my revenge. I assured them I would think on it during my trip. I swore the pair to secrecy, and we locked forearms in the vow.

The news of my return to St. Petersburg preceded me by several days, via post. Chatter being what it was in the capital, old Viktor could not have been uninformed of my continued state of good health. Upon arrival, I bruited it about that poor Petrovski had fallen overboard during a storm and been lost. Times being as rough as they were and having heard nothing of the fate of his amber cutter, if I were Protopopov I would have believed that his hired assassins had taken the money given to them for murder and simply vanished. At any rate, when Viktor spied me in the cold, windswept street soon after my return he showed no surprise.

That night, I had a vision of the three white-robed attackers, appearing as if ghosts. This was closely followed by the appearance of my father, as he looked just before he died. I expected that he would be as mute as he had been in his final days. Instead, he whispered a short sentence that both rattled and elated me. During my many travels, I had read Shakespeare's great play, *Hamlet*. It also had the elements of ghosts and a father communicating with his son from beyond the grave. I wondered for many days thereafter whether or not what I had experienced was a mere dream or a visitation. In truth, it hardly mattered; either way, it set me on a path to certain revenge.

On the twelfth day of December, with the season's seventh snowfall – ice puddles dappling the streets, and icicles hanging like legions of Damocles' sword from building eaves – the old wolf waddled into our offices and immediately demanded a cup of tea. The moment we were alone, he noted that I seemed to have developed far more interest in porcelain than amber and offered to buy out our mine and offices "…so that you may have the money to corner the market on china in Moscow and St. Petersburg." His price was almost fair. I told him that I would have to think on the offer, needing time to assess future markets and so forth. He made me promise that, in the event I did elect to quit the amber business, he be allowed to make the final offer. I acquiesced and he shambled out the door, quaking and cursing the instant the cold touched his face.

Days dragged into weeks. Russian winter, the stepbrother of Death itself, sat hard upon the land, invading our homes and our beds, searching out the life-warmth of our very marrows. Eventually, spring of 1722 slid smoothly in over the last of the ice, bringing with it an astonishing rumor. The tsar, who just proclaimed himself emperor in celebration of his triumph over the Swedes via the peace of Nystad, was proposing a revolutionary change to the order of nobility. No longer would people be promoted in the state services based purely on ancestral lineage. All functionary offices were to be categorized into fourteen levels, fourteen being lowest and one the highest. The eighth level conferred hereditary nobility, regardless of blood lines. Rank was assigned based on one's services to the regime. Therefore, the owner of an important factory might, in effect, receive blue blood status. So might an indispensable amber merchant. Most importantly, the edict provided the final element I needed to destroy Viktor Protopopov.

As well as learning from departed Scandinavian edda bards, Greek moralists, French philosophers and English playwrights, I had read a history of Rodrigo Borgia and the magnum opus of the diplomat Machiavelli. Under the warm skies of Italy, the Italians had cultivated revenge to an art form. Their invariably effective ways were so famous that their word vendetta had crept into several other European languages. Similarly, their admonition on how to execute vendetta had been passed on with utmost respect: Revenge is a dish best served cold. This, of course, meant figuratively that one is capable of committing far greater harm when one's anger has subsided, a response can be more thoughtfully designed, and the victim has become more likely to have lowered his or her guard. I, however, took the advice literally.

Old Protopopov had already expended vast amounts of capital underwriting social events and on the outward trappings of wealth to gain a grudging acceptance among the lower ranks of St. Petersburg society. When I finally accepted his purchase proposal, albeit at twenty percent more than he had originally offered, he leapt at the opportunity. How else would such a mind think other than "The temporary depletion of almost all my wealth will quickly be outweighed by the bestowing of Level Eight to our house, as the monopolistic controller of amber."

The continued costs in currying the favor of the middle and upper nobles, however, was more costly than the old wolf had anticipated. The clamor for amber had faded, replaced by other newly fashionable expressions of wealth. Within two years, Protopopov was forced to sell his amber monopoly to me…at half its value. He maintained his title. But, as they say, "You can't eat title."

Nevertheless, one must eat. In his eagerness to emulate the truly rich, Viktor had squandered a fortune on a sixty-four-piece setting of gold dishes.

The problem is that gold is a demon at conducting heat away, robbing the food upon it of warmth even before the servants can get it to the table. The Old Guard, who grew up with gold plates, never knew anything else and never missed the delight of hot food. But I, obeying the Italian admonition, had deprived Viktor Ivanovitch Protopopov of what he had so often declared "the only joy left in my life." As a final insult to his shivering bulk, the demi-palace he had built to impress the nobles had a dining room too fancy for open-faced fireplaces. I was told by noble friends who so love to enjoy the misery of others, that the huge room was like "a stable in the dead of winter."

The night I heard for certain the voice of my ghost father. The words sounded hollow, yet they were distinct: "Make him even colder." I had wondered for a brief spell if my father was urging his rival's murder. But I quickly remembered that he had been a temperate man all his life and would never have counseled violence as a solution. So, instead, I bided my time and used Viktor's greatest weaknesses against him. By the time old Protopopov was forced to sell the gold plates and could not afford even porcelain, the tiny glowing cinder that had substituted so long for a heart had burned out, trapped in permanent ice. Like an insect in amber.

Blood Drive

CHAPTER ONE – April

ACROSS THE CAMPUS GREENS of Philadelphia's Stratford College, spring was coming into full bloom. In the office of the Dean of Student Life, the ambience was perpetual winter.

"No matter how many times we lecture you, no matter how often we send our sororities and fraternities warnings against hazing," Dean Abigail Myers lectured, "it persists."

Samantha Martin noted well the dean's body language from her seat on the visitor side of the impressive cherry wood desk. Myers' right eyebrow was cocked, her glossless lips were puckered into two thin slits between sentences and her arms were folded over her flat chest. The thought flashed through Sam's mind that Myers would not in a million years have been invited to join Sigma Epsilon Chi.

Sam leaned slightly forward, calculating what would express confidence without crossing the line to cockiness. "I assure you, Dean Myers, that our initiation rites are the farthest thing from making pledges drink to the point of alcohol poisoning or blindfolding them and letting them walk off cliffs. We are responsible young women."

"And yet we have one of your pledges in the clinic with acute dermatitis," Myers countered.

Sam affixed her best sober face and nodded. "And we're all extremely sorry. But what are the chances, really, that Madison would be allergic to one of the ingredients in the wax?"

Myers continued to scowl. "It's not that alone. This mishap exposed shocking behavior on the part of your members. Forcing pledges to display their private parts would be deemed a criminal act outside of the campus."

The Sigma Epsilon Chi president sighed lightly. "Well, that's simply choosing to look on what we did the wrong way. You walk around the campus every day. You see how many of Stratford's coeds look just like their grandmothers did at Woodstock. Rescue Mission clothing, purposely faded and torn. Scalps looking like they sleep in barns. Unibrows, hair in their armpits long enough to French braid and pubic hair the size of eagles' nests down below. It's a definite turnoff, especially to the nice young men who want to date them. Brazilian waxing is part of good grooming nowadays. Like powder and rouge when Stratford first opened."

To provide visual punctuation to her argument, Sam crossed her epilated left leg over her opposite knee, revealing four-inch, open-toed tacones. She took a calculated moment to flatten her flower-print skirt primly over her shapely ankle. Abigail Myers, in her mid-fifties, was unmarried and rumored to have a secret partner who was a faculty member at U. of Penn.

The dean flushed slightly but maintained her stern expression. "It's no secret that the board of trustees wants to abolish Greek life at this college. Ever since that incident at Tau Kappa Mu."

The fraternity's brothers had hatched the idea of bringing their pledges one at a time up to the frat house's flat roof and asking them to estimate how far it was to the ground. After the guess was made, they tied one end of a length of cord to a cinder block, measured out the pledge's estimate and tied the other end around his exposed penis and testicles. Then they heaved the cinder block over the edge. In reality, they had allowed an extra three feet of cord beyond the actual distance. However, one time the cinder block struck at such an angle that it rolled over twice. The pledge suffered groin injuries requiring surgery.

"That was disgusting," Samantha said with vehemence. "The administration was right to shut that house down. As chapter president, I take great offense over Sigma Ep being compared with them. In fact, if you are called to speak to the board of trustees about us, we wish you would mention the fall charity run we organized for victims of syringomyelia. Also, the blood drive we're coordinating among six sororities on different Philadelphia college campuses next October."

"I hadn't heard of the latter," Myers admitted.

Sam expected the response, since she and Mary, the house's VP-elect for their senior year and Sam's best friend, had only devised the drive directly after Madison Sizemore developed the blisters all around her genital area.

"Absolutely. Our chapter works diligently to develop responsible members of society," Sam affirmed. As she watched the dean's facial muscles relax, she wondered what Myers would have thought of the GoPro camera she had hidden before the hazing session, for the later enjoyment of Bobby Northrup, her boyfriend and leading wide receiver of the Stratford football team.

CHAPTER TWO – October

"This thing cost more than $3,000! Why can't it tell me the day and time?" house vice president, Mary Pendergast, complained, glaring at the Cartier watch on her left wrist.

Samantha Martin sighed. "Because you asked your daddy for the wrong style. Just consider it fine jewelry and consult your iPhone for the time. It's October 2nd, Turdlette. As in Blood Drive Day."

"Which we are walking to as we speak," Mary defended. "I just forgot the date."

The Stratford coeds crossed the central green carrying nothing in their arms and wearing only chic fanny packs. "Clayton better have brought everything to the Bloodmobile," Sam said. "I keep reminding him that he owes us permanently for having the classiest fag hag friends in school." She waved to a female student walking toward them. "Hey, Janet! You are donating to the blood drive today, aren't you?"

Janet Evans slowed her pace. "I have a cold. I can't give."

"Quel dommage, Cheri!" Sam returned with effusion. "But surely you'll be over it in time to donate at Temple or U. of Penn. Check the days and locations in the *Daily Bard*. Mary and I are in charge of coordination and record keeping, so we'll expect to see your name on the donation rolls by October 26th."

"Two pints expected from Janet-come-latelies!" Mary chirped. "Only kidding! But remember that one sister from each campus will win two tickets to the fabulous Haunted House of Horror Sig Ep is hosting on Halloween evening. All other donors who want to attend pay a reasonable fee." Janet walked on without comment. Mary called after her, "And it's a costume party. A pair of Eagles tickets for best costume." Janet did not reply. "Bitch," Mary muttered.

The Red Cross Bloodmobile was parked in the exact center of Stratford's campus.

While they were still at a distance, Sam said, "Well, at least Clayton came through. There's his rainbow LGBTQIA+ banner."

"Well, that ought to kill the drive," Mary remarked. "It's not as if gays and blood conjure up happy thoughts. More like Tom Hanks in Philadelphia."

"What could we do?" Sam returned. "He's one of our closest friends. And our sorority doesn't need high numbers to keep from being shut down. 'It's the thought that counts.'"

"Tell that to all the people who desperately need transfusions."

"Pardon me, Clara Barton."

"Count the crowd, Blood Clot!"

As Sam approached the setup, she counted two donors sitting on folding chairs, sipping from little cups of orange juice. Two other students filled out the required forms. Beside the donors stood a middle-aged female nurse and two men Sam judged to be in their mid to late twenties. Both were good looking and well built.

Clayton spotted the sorority president and VP. He grabbed a clipboard and strode toward them.

"Doesn't he have anything but cowboy duds in his wardrobe?" Mary asked, through ventriloquist lips, looking at their friend's Frye boots, Levi jeans, thick belt with a Longhorn steer brass buckle, plaid flannel shirt, black neckerchief and black Stetson ten-gallon hat.

Through a warm smile, Sam replied, "Not much. Ever since he was told at age six that he has the same first name as the actor who played the Lone Ranger on TV, he's been fixated on cowboys. Dani told me he likes to ride her wearing nothing but boots, spurs and chaps."

"Too much information," Mary said.

"You asked about his wardrobe."

"How goes it, Sisters?" Clayton asked, in his macho bass voice.

"You tell us," Mary invited.

"Kinda slow. Eight so far…counting me."

Sam refused to contribute to the conversation. She had expected a less-than-booming response from the Stratford population. Those not in fraternities and sororities generally dismissed the Greek life as outdated and exclusive. This was especially true of Sigma Ep, which had the most well-off women and the deserved reputation of being stuck-up bitches. Ergo, a goodly number of the frat brothers and other house sisters would also boycott the effort. And then there was the co-sponsorship of the LGBTQIA+ club, which was derided and looked down on by the ignorant.

"Ten soon, with you two," Clayton added.

"Must be the campus epidemic of genital warts," Sam said loudly, directing her words at a group of four women walking past and doing their best not to see the bloodmobile. "Clayton, do you know the difference between true love and herpes?"

"No, dear. What's the difference between true love and herpes?"

"Herpes is forever," Sam snickered. Dropping back into seriousness she growled, "Well, every damned Sig Ep sister and their beaux had better show up here today," said Sam. She looked past Clayton. "What's the story with the two hunks?"

"Rod and Tony? Both straight," Clayton supplied. "They've dumped charm on every female who's approached." He rolled his eyes. "But looks and fast talk aren't everything. How much can a bloodmobile technician earn? I say they're capitalizing on a non-threatening way to meet women. They must get into more vaginas than Tampax."

Samantha and Mary were introduced first to the formidable nurse in charge of the operation and then to Rod Cooper and Tony Enescu. Both looked to be in their late twenties and were indeed very cute. Rod was the taller and thinner of the two, with curly hair tinged with red. Tony was darker skinned, with thick chestnut hair that came to a widow's peak and a broad, toothy smile. As Clayton had promised, they chatted Sam and Mary up the whole time the coeds filled out their donation forms. Tony's grammar and vocabulary were normal, but he spoke with the hint of an accent, which he said was Yugoslavian. He told the women that he had been in the United States since he was ten.

Sam showed her identification and glanced at a pamphlet on donating blood. She provided her current address and began answering questions on eligibility. She paused at the next-to-last question, then glanced at the large sign on the table that had a cartoon of smiling, short, medium and tall, old and young, Negro, Asian and European men and woman linking hands. The slogan below read: ALL TYPES WELCOME!

"Type? I have no idea. I've never given blood."

"Me neither," Mary echoed.

"No problem," Rod assured. "We always sample a drop from each donor. We can send you the information later, on a card you should keep in your wallet. Should it be in care of the sorority you have listed here?"

"Right." Sam scrunched up her face. "Is this gonna hurt?"

"I will do my very best to see that it doesn't," Rod said. "There's a trick of pinching up your skin as I insert the needle, so you feel nothing more than the pressure."

"A skilled blood sucker, eh?" Sam joked.

"The word is phlebotomist," Rod replied.

CHAPTER THREE

Samantha Martin was a word person. Numbers had always been the bane of her existence. Even balancing her checking and debit card accounts were too much for her, which she used as the excuse for being overdrawn so often. Stratford College required each student to take at least one mathematics course as part of the core curriculum, and the least difficult elective past her high school algebra and geometry was trigonometry. A coed named Ginger Ross, who was a member of Delta Zeta, was also enrolled in the class and shared Sam's antipathy and low grades. Misery loving company, they sat next to each other during lectures.

The grad student teaching the course was scribbling a formula on the whiteboard as Sam entered the hall. She plopped herself down onto her usual seat with a sigh.

"I'm a fiction writing major. This is an expensive, worthless waste of my time."

"Amen," Ginger muttered in sympathy.

"Why can't this class be about love triangles instead?" Sam complained.

"I'm good at those," Ginger said.

Sam's attention focused. "Say what? Spill already."

Ginger smiled wickedly. "You know I've been dating Eddie Carabelli since November."

"But –"

"But that guy from the blood drive – Tony E. – wouldn't stop calling me. Six calls in four days."

Sam was frankly amazed by the news. Ginger was not only faulty of face and flat of figure, but she also had poor fashion sense. Attracting Eddie Carabelli was one thing. He looked to Sam like he had been chasing parked cars. But the handsome, well-built phlebotomist was way above Ginger's dating class. "And?"

"So, I'm two-timing Frankie on the sly. Just for variety's sake. I mean, Tony's bloodmobile covers Bucks, Berks, Philadelphia, Montgomery and Chester counties. He's gone by the end of the month from this neck of the woods."

"Have you hooked up?" Sam asked.

"Not yet. I don't put out until the third date," Ginger affirmed. "Frankie's team will be playing an away game in Pittsburgh Halloween weekend, so I invited Tony to the party. Him and his partner, Rod, as well. That spooky mansion, with all its bedrooms, should be a hell of a place to get laid. And then Tony's gone, and it's back to reliable Eddie."

"The two blood takers will cost you an extra sixty bucks, Big Spender," Sam said.

"No biggie. My dad will write it off to charity."

The grad student teacher closed the door to the hall and focused unhappily on her apathetic class.

Ginger said, "I never asked you how many donated on our campus?"

Samantha opened her notebook. "A hundred and nine."

"Over two days? That's pathetic, even for a small college."

"Yeah, well, iGens may drink less and be more racially, sexually and religiously tolerant, but self-sacrificing they're not," Sam defended, well aware that she was talking about herself, her sorority sisters and other friends. "The bloodmobile's at

Temple today through Friday. I bet they get at least 400 pints."

"I'll be sure to ask Tony Friday night," Ginger said.

CHAPTER FOUR

Samantha closed the book she was reading and pushed her bottom back in the Adirondack chair as she watched Mary climb the steps to the porch of Sigma Epsilon Chi.

"Hey, Whore," she greeted. "What's your problem? Somebody run over your pet pussy?" Then she noticed that what she thought was merely a lack of expression on Mary's face was actually a cloud of grimness.

"Shut up, Troll!" Mary returned. She plopped herself down on another of the motley grouping of chairs that had accumulated as bequests over the years. "I just came back from Delta Psi Delta."

Sam knew that Mary was supposed to visit Villanova University that afternoon, to coordinate the decorating of the mansion that lay at the tail end of Philadelphia's Main Line. The fourteen-acre estate, with its empty, enormous Victorian monstrosity at the center, had been the major item in an inheritance battle for years and had been allowed to fall into ruin by its eccentric owner for a decade before that. Sam's plan for linking a Halloween costume bash with the blood drive had been embraced by the women of $\Delta\Psi\Delta$ at Villanova and $\Gamma\Phi\Lambda$ at La Salle University. A total of twelve tickets had been awarded at the six donating colleges as prizes, and ninety four more sold, to pay for the alcohol, DJ and decorations.

"Don't tell me their boyfriends are chickening out on cutting the chain on the back gate," Sam worried.

"No," Mary replied, in a sober tone. "One of their sisters was killed last night."

Sam's head reared back. "Murdered?"

"No. Nothing that simple."

"Well, what?"

"She had her head separated from her body at the neck. By one of those steel guy-wires that hold up telephone poles."

"Shit. Way bizarre"

Mary nodded. "Tell me about it. Brittany Somebody. She gave a pint of her blood for their drive last week. She was seen drinking at My Lost Lenore around ten-thirty. One of the bartenders said she was picked up by a good-looking guy with a baseball cap that had 'Liga 1' stitched on it." Mary pronounced the word like the first two syllables of "ligament."

"What's Liga 1? A craft beer?"

"I have no idea. They left together on his Harley."

Sam set down the history book, an authoritative resource on the French and Indian Wars. Lackadaisical about virtually every other course subject, when she got an idea for her fiction writing class she went about her research with fanatical drive. She believed that the more realism she included, the easier it was for her readers to suspend their disbelief and enjoy the vicarious ride. "If the Harley were hers, I could understand. She's drunk; it was raining last night; she hits a pothole or a puddle and goes off the road; she doesn't see the wire, hits it at high speed and decapitates herself. But no guy is gonna let a woman he picks up in a bar pilot his hog while he rides shotgun."

Mary sighed. "Traces of blood on the wire and her body in weeds fifty feet beyond. They said she lost pretty much every platelet in her body, even though they didn't find much blood. Must have washed away in the rain. No 'cycle. No brake or skid marks. No good-looking guy in a cap. No accident reported."

"Did she have tickets to the Haunted House of Horror?"

"I didn't ask."

"Bummer," Sam decided. "But I tell you what a real bummer will be: if those Villanova guys back out on cutting that chain."

CHAPTER FIVE

"Ginger Ross? What the F!" Mary shrieked from atop her bed. Sam had entered her friend's room two moments before. "How?"

"In her car. That beat-up Camaro of hers," Sam said. "Straight across a T intersection in Fishtown and into a stone wall. Total incineration. I heard the corpse looked like Cajun ribs from head to toe. Clothes burnt completely off. Hair gone."

"Was she alone?"

"If she wasn't, her passengers got out safe and sound and fled the scene." Then Sam's face went slack. "Wait a second. Last night was Friday."

"Duh. And you say I never know what day it is," Mary mocked.

"Ginger told me she was going out with that guy from the bloodmobile on Friday night. Tony E."

"Yeah. The one with the accent."

"And Ginger gave blood the same day we did."

"Double duh."

"Like that Delta Psi Delta sister from Villanova. Brittany Barrett."

"She didn't give blood with us," Mary said.

"No, Moron. She gave blood at Villanova. And she died after meeting some guy nobody knew at My Lost Lenore."

"Coincidence," Mary decided. She looked hard at her friend. "Did you just shiver?"

Sam ignored the question and sat at Mary's desk. "Do you still have the clipboard Sammy used to record our donors and their information?"

"Yeah. Also copies of the donor lists from the other five schools. Under that stack of *Cosmos* and *Vogues*. Why?"

Sam unburied the board and ran her finger down the list until she reached Ginger Ross. "I wonder if Ginger and Brittany both dated that same guy with the baseball cap."

"Oh, think straight, Sam," Mary chided. "What's the chance of that?"

CHAPTER SIX

The Barry estate lay well hidden from passing traffic, behind hundred-year-old stands of trees that were vibrantly red, yellow and orange in the dying light of All Hallow's Evening. Boyfriends of party-going ΔΨΔ sisters had cut the chain looped through the estate's rear gate, allowing dozens of cars, pickups and motorcycles onto the property.

The drive looped past what had once been a six-horse stable and fed into a turn-around that ran under the mansion's porte cochere. The structure was formidable from all angles. It was fashioned of granite stone that had darkened unevenly over many decades, but the most unnerving aspect was the lack of any light emanating from its window openings. Every space had been blocked with half-inch plywood screwed into the walls to defend against vandalizing. Perhaps to prevent warping and swelling from humidity, all the plywood had been painted a lacquer black on the outside. Sam's last boyfriend, Bobby Northrup, a jock BMOC and son of a local family, had found the perfect venue for a frightening Halloween.

Both Sam and Mary had been dumped in late September. The guys they had stolen from other women the previous year had both fled in favor of the latest crop of freshwomen, beauties blinded by the excitement of dating popular seniors. Walking side by side toward the mansion from Mary's late-model Mustang, the pair's lack of hunky squires had put both in a foul mood.

"Look back in those trees," Mary said. "A motorcycle."

Sam changed course. "Let's check it out."

What was chained to one of the trees was a Harley-Davidson Road King in black. It was nearly invisible among the unlit trees.

"Ya think?" Mary asked.

"Don't go weak-kneed on me, Turd. Let's ask around."

"Who arrived on the motorcycle?" Sam asked a pair of her sorority sisters who sat on the mansion veranda, collecting tickets and returning prize-drawing stubs.

Both shrugged. "I heard it but didn't see it," reported a sophomore named Breezy, whose buck teeth were accentuated by the fact that she had dressed as the White Rabbit from Alice in Wonderland. Co-doorkeeper Ashley concurred, in a voice that echoed within the inverted fishbowl that served as her Martian helmet.

"What's the count?" Sam said.

"Sixty," Ashley answered.

"Sixty?" Mary consulted her diamond-chip-studded Cartier watch. "It's twenty to nine. We gave away twelve and sold a hundred-something more!" She had dressed like Glinda from The Wizard of Oz and shook her electrified magic wand up and down angrily.

"We think people were scared away by the deaths of two of our donors," Breezy replied. "You do have to admit it's way creepy." As she spoke, she flipped through a small box, plucked out two cards that held stick-on name tags for Mary and Sam, and handed them over. Underneath each name was printed their blood type. Sam's was A positive, and Mary's was O negative.

Sam was dressed from mop-cut hairdo to booted toes exactly as Milla Jovovitch's character, Alice, in the *Resident Evil* film series, including black leather bodice bristling with straps and a pair of hip-hugging pistols.

Sam turned a full circle in her annoyance, slapping the name tag onto her chest as she pivoted. "Jesus wept! No good deed goes unpunished. Well, that much more booze to take back to the house."

"Those guns aren't real, are they?" Ashley asked.

"Hell if they aren't," Sam spat back. "I bought this rig at the gun show last week. What good is having no waiting period or background checks if you don't buy a pair of deadly Sig Sauer P226s?"

Ashley and Breezy stared at Sam, not sure if their president was kidding or not.

Sam thrust out her right hand. "Give me the bedrooms sign-up kit!" While she waited, she said to Mary "Let's make sure everything else is running smoothly." They passed through the mansion's overlarge iron front doors that looked like they could withstand a battering ram.

Like a commanding general with her adjutant beside her, Sam conducted a last-minute walkthrough of the appropriated house. The main festive areas and spaces best illuminated were the huge foyer, a two-story-high library to its right, and a dining room to its left that had once held a table Huck and Jim could have poled down the Mississippi on. The DJ had set up his equipment in the library. The room's only remaining owner articles were lines of books on shelves too high to reach. Toward the rear of the first floor lay the kitchen, pantry, smoking parlor and billiard room. The second floor held seven bedrooms and a nanny's quarters, with abundant closets and bathrooms. The cellar had never been finished but was a ready-made maze of dead-end spaces and corridors. Electricity had long since been shut off, necessitating the importation of scores of candles and a dozen spotlights run by battery power. The DJ had brought his own lighting, hooked up to car batteries. The organizers had also rounded up a couple dozen flashlights for use in moving among the corridors and rooms. Several filled galvanized buckets stood next to each of the mansion's toilets, since the water had also been shut off.

Mary and Sam moved through the gloom of the barely lit upstairs hallway, pinning onto each of the bedroom doors sign-up sheets that reserved each space for thirty minutes, on the hour and half-hour, and providing pencils that hung from cotton twine.

"Hotel California" boomed across the foyer, and strobe lights whirled, as Mary and Sam completed their inspection tour.

"Talk about fashionably late!" Clayton called out through the gyrating throng. He dragged a mesmerizingly beautiful creature along behind him. Clayton's partner, who was named Dani, had chosen to wear an abbreviated version of the wicked stepmother costume from Disney's *Snow White*. Down to the waist, the look was identical: but the voluminous, black silk skirts had been cut away in the front to show off Dani's perfectly turned legs and black-sequined, four-inch high heels. A glittering faux-diamond choker circled her long neck.

Dani flashed a perfect smile and wriggled her fingers in greeting.

"I begged her to come as Tonto," Clayton announced, "but she's allergic to feathers."

Clayton beamed with joy at having the opportunity to display the exact duplicate of the Lone Ranger outfit Clayton Moore had worn for the 1950's television series. His bluish-grey shirt and pants combination provided the background for a brilliant red neckerchief, black gloves and mask, white Stetson and a pair of matching six guns in holsters, held tight against his thighs by drawstrings. The black gun belt was circled by some two-dozen spare bullets held within leather loops. Gleaming leather riding boots completed the ensemble.

"You'll win the prize hands down," Sam judged. "You clearly didn't get all this at Party City."

"I ordered pieces from all over the Southwest," Clayton shared. "Cost me a small fortune."

"As if your allowance isn't a small fortune," Sam rejoined.

"Thriller" pulsed out of the DJ's speakers.

Dani pointed to her tag. "This isn't my blood type. Should I fix it?"

"No," Sam replied. "It's not important."

Sam's gaze shifted to the bottom of the main staircase, where a makeshift bar had been set up in the curve. Three beer kegs sat on a table made from a thick plywood panel and sawhorses. Around the area sat more than a dozen portable plastic coolers, from which partiers were taking bottled craft brew and ice. As she focused on the scene, the two blood drive technicians appeared from the back of the house.

"The probable owner of the Harley," Mary muttered.

"Courage, Glinda," Sam said, as she pulled Mary toward the men. Even before she reached them, she began speaking. "Hi, guys! Using Ginger's tickets?"

"That we are," replied Tony Enescu, taking in the president's superhero outfit. "Ginger gave them to me to hold onto."

"The night she died," Sam supplied.

"Exactly right." Tony changed his expression to that of mixed sadness and disbelief and slowly shook his head. "What a terrible tragedy."

"How was it she was alone in her car?"

"We agreed to meet at Murph's Bar. I thought we really hit it off, but when I suggested she come back to my motel room, she gave me the stiff arm. We chatted for another half hour, and then she left."

"Was she drunk?"

"I didn't think so. Otherwise, I wouldn't have let her get in her car."

Sam glanced at Tony's tag. "O positive" had been written in Magic Marker under his name.

"I thought you'd get a lot more takers than this," Rod admitted. He had assembled a piss-poor excuse for a pirate costume, with his curly, russet hair hidden under a paisley bandanna, a soccer sweatshirt with horizon black and white stripes, black trousers rolled halfway up his ankles, no socks and black loafers. What looked genuine were the lethal-looking hook covering his right hand and the broadsword tucked into the red sash running around his waist.

Tony's getup was pure Bela Lugosi as Dracula, including the high-collared, flowing cape.

"With that widow's peak of yours, the Werewolf would have worked better," Sam judged.

"Nah," Tony answered. "I prefer this."

Suddenly, over the din of the DJ's music, the foyer echoed with the clang of the front doors being slammed. Two Sigma Ep boyfriends, one wearing a mummy outfit and the other dressed as The Amazing Hulk, leaned against the doors and crossed their arms in a forbidding manner.

"Nine o'clock on the nose," Mary announced, consulting her wristwatch by the flickering light of a candelabra.

Sam raised her hands and turned slowly as she spoke, taking in the entire crowd. "Welcome to the Halloween Haunted House of Horror. Any of you lowlife guys who have already drunk too much and were planning on watering the bushes outside, it's too late. Those doors are sealed until midnight." She nodded toward the door guards. From his waist, the larger of the pair unwrapped a length of chain and began to ceremoniously pass it through and around the door handles several times. "We don't want any faint-hearted chickenshits running from the house prematurely, just because they encounter some scary moments. Especially downstairs…in the Maze of Madness."

The crowd laughed.

"But, in case of an emergency, either Chris or Jack will be near the doors with…"

The larger guard produced an oversize lock, which he snapped shut through two links of the chain.

"…the combination to that lock."

From out of the crowd came a ghostly "WOOOOOO!" This time, the laughter had a slight edge.

"Remember that alcohol and flame don't mix well," Sam went on, "so be especially aware of the candles. Most are battery-operated, but –" She pointed to the sixteen flames directly above her in the chandelier. "– some are live. Have a scary, but safe, evening."

The crowd began to disperse, in pairs and small groupings.

"You know, you're absolutely nuts, Sam," Mary said, as Tony and Rod moved to the bar to pour Chablis into plastic wine glasses. "They both go out in daylight. Obviously, they both…drink 'vine'," she added, doing her best Lugosi imitation.

"And yet there's a Harley outside. And you're afraid to cozy up to them," Sam said.

Mary's hand inched toward the gold cross that hung from a chain around her neck. "What if your crazy idea is true? What could be a better job for vampires than working a bloodmobile?"

"But it's the 'why' that's important," Sam emphasized. "If it only came down to needing human blood to exist, they could prey indiscriminately on an entire world of victims. But Ginger and Brittany both had negative blood types."

"What's the total percentage of people with negative blood again?" Mary asked.

"A-, AB-, B- and O-negative combined add up to only fifteen percent of the population. Not even a sixth."

"Including me."

"So, their jobs are perfect, because they know exactly who among the donors are negatives before they attack them. The evidence suggests that vampires – or at least these two bloodsuckers – can only tolerate negative types."

"You came up with this hare-brained idea purely based on Ginger and Brittany."

Rod waved at Sam from a distance. She smiled and returned the gesture. "Suspected but later corroborated. Brittany was – as you yourself said – virtually drained dry of blood and Ginger was so cremated that no one could tell if she had been. Actually, I've been holding out on you, just to make sure you didn't back out. You know how much research I do when I get an idea for my fiction writing."

"Yeah?"

"Well, I got from the Eastern Pennsylvania chapter of the Red Cross the travel schedule of their bloodmobile for the past year. During that period, I found nineteen suspicious accidents that resulted in the death of a person who had donated to that bloodmobile shortly before. For all I know, there might have been fifty more. In most cases, it was impossible to get their blood types."

"No doubt."

Sam leaned closer to Mary. "But for the five I did get, four had negative types. Take that deer in the headlights look off your face and give Tony a smile, Mare."

Mary obliged with some effort. "So, how do we prove your theory?"

"Neither of them had access to the attendee list for this party, but they knew at least half of us gave blood during the drive. They no doubt have their donor lists from the six colleges. Lists with the individual blood types. All they need to do is follow one or two of the negatives after the party in order to get another Happy Meal."

"Whoa!" Mary exhaled.

"Bad Moon Rising" filled the library and foyer.

Sam said, "Just in case, I made it even easier for them to home in on prey."

"You had Breezy put everyone's blood type under their names on the tags."

"Bazinga. Plus, I've recruited Chris, Marina, Jack, Cheryl, Clayton and Dani to help us tail the two of them. I gave them a bullshit story about Rod and Tony being robbers and rapists, but the truth will come out."

Mary glanced down at her tag. "And I'm –"

"Bloody Mary, prime decoy. Time to dilute your negative cells with some wine, Sister."

"Thanks a bunch, Twat. While Rod and Tony are doing their midnight shopping."

Sam whispered in Mary's ear. "Not only do I have real bullets in my pistols, but Clayton's revolvers are also loaded. Have no fear."

"Look! They disappeared. Where did they go?" Mary wondered.

"Probably making their list and checking it twice. Relax. With all these people here, they can't do anything until after the party." Sam drained her drink. "Let's get some of the harder stuff from the ice chests and then walk through the Maze of Madness."

President and VP descended to the basement, bumping into other partiers in the dimness. Sitting alone on a lower step was Rod sipping from his plastic wine glass. He stood as the two women descended.

"Shiver me timbers, if it isn't the two most beautiful wenches on this island!" he exclaimed. "Do ye mind if I meander the maze with ye?"

"If you lead the way," Sam said.

The cellar, which ran the length and width of the house, had been divided haphazardly over the years into many storage rooms. To prevent the revelers from wandering forever, various means of blockading doors and passages had been assembled to establish a set route. Because the maze was to be used only one night, darkness more than frightening elements provided the mood. Plastic skeletons had been shackled to walls; fake spider webs had been sprayed to tangle in hair; bats dangled and spun lazily from the first floor joists; a human shape lay under a sheet on a picnic table, its right hand constantly twitching; ghost heads fashioned from balloons trapped under white gauze bounced up and down from behind moldy boxes and crates. One sister's engineering student boyfriend had rigged up invisible electric beams that triggered sudden loud noises, strobe flashes of light, and a full-size gorilla figure that swung into the path of oncoming visitors.

In two locations, around right-angle turns, full-length mirrors had been set up to reflect the approaching maze goers. Each time, Rod pretended to duel with his image. While he battled and hurled verbal challenges on the second encounter, Mary whispered to Sam, "Not invisible in the glass."

"Hey, I'm more than happy to be wrong," Sam replied softly.

Near the end of the maze lay a room that appeared empty except for an axe lying on the stone floor in a pool of blood. Mary shone her flashlight on it.

"That looks like real blood," she decided.

"And a real axe," Rod added. He ventured into the room and knelt beside the axe. He dipped the middle finger of the hand without the hook lightly into the liquid. "It has the consistency of blood." He moved his hand into Mary's beam of light. "And the color." Then his gaze shifted, and he sprang backward, landing on his behind, causing his cutlass to clang against the floor. "Is that real?" he yelped.

Sam swung around the door and looked behind it. Lying face up was a figure wearing a Donald Trump mask, a blue suit and a red tie. Sam had seen the costume upstairs only minutes before. And then she realized that the figure mostly hid another one lying behind it, that of a girl whose hair was arranged like that of Melania Trump. Both had been struck hard in their necks and were covered with blood.

"Don't touch that!" Mary ordered Rod, who had reached out to the axe's haft. "Fingerprints."

Rod nodded and stood. He reached into a trouser pocket. "I'm calling 911."

Upstairs, over the pounding beats of "Ghostbusters," echoed a faint but piercing scream.

Sam grabbed Mary's arm and dragged her roughly and quickly up the cellar steps and into the foyer area. Just as they reached the center of the space, a sorority sister from La Salle, dressed like a nurse, appeared at the top of the main staircase to the upper floor. Blood covered her hands, arms, and the hem of her uniform.

"There are two dead people in the master bedroom!" she yelled down to the crowd. She pointed behind her needlessly, as her partner, dressed like a doctor, with a stethoscope around his neck and the zipper of his trousers down, backed into view. He collided with the nurse. She screamed, causing several other women below to imitate her.

"Ghostbusters" segued into "Dead Man's Party."

"Shut up, everyone!" Sam commanded. "Stay calm! Let's all exit onto the porch and take a head count."

"Where's Chris?" Mary asked anxiously, speaking of one of the door guards.

The girl in the nurse's uniform cried out, "He's in the master bedroom. Dead!"

More and more partiers rushed into the foyer and onto the balcony at the top of the staircase. With each passing second, their panic grew.

"Stay calm!" Sam cried out. "Where's Jack?"

Everyone looked around. When it became apparent that the second doorkeeper was absent, a half dozen of the male attendees rushed to the great iron doors and began tugging at the chained handles. Several others attempted to rip away the thick plywood that covered the windows on either side of the doors. As their combined impotence became apparent to all, a wail issued in unison from dozens of throats.

"What happened to the cutter you guys used to break the rear road chain?" Sam asked.

"It's in my pickup," one of the Villanova students said.

"Naturally," Sam muttered.

"I can't get reception!" Rod cried out loudly, holding up his cell phone.

The uproar softened a bit as dozens of mobile phones appeared, their combined lights brightening the foyer.

"Mine either!" voice after voice said.

"Everyone gather in the front three rooms!" Sam ordered. "There's safety in numbers and plenty of light. Where's Clayton?"

"Here!" the Masked Rider of the Plains called out, appearing from the dining room.

"You and Dani, Mary and I will check the rooms upstairs, to see that everyone's out of them."

"I'll come with you," Rod volunteered.

Sam smiled. "Good idea." To the sophomore who had been screaming and who was now hyperventilating, she asked, "Which room?"

The girl, whose name tag read Nancy and whose blood type was O positive, pointed. "Luh, luh, left," she managed.

Sam climbed the first four staircase steps and turned to address the close-packed crowd. "The rest of you see if you can find anything that can pry the wood off the windows. Move in groups of no fewer than three!"

When Sam and Molly had checked the second floor on their tour, the central corridor had been lit with more than a dozen electric candles set in holders on the floor, as well as 12v emergency light units at either end of the house. Now, every one of the sources of illumination had disappeared.

"Feeling brave, Rod?" Sam asked.

"Not especially," he replied. "But give me your flashlight."

"No, I'll hold onto it," she said. "That's a real sword, isn't it?"

"It is."

Rod advanced slowly down the left wing, with Sam behind him. Clayton, Mary, and Dani ventured a little way down the right side of the corridor, relying on two flashlights and the faint light shining up from the foyer.

"Why do you trust me so much?" Rod asked, over his shoulder.

"Who says I do?"

"You just told everyone not to travel in groups smaller than three."

"But I have loaded pistols, and you have that big sword," Sam said, placing her thumb around her right gun and moving her forefinger to release the safety. "Besides, we might momentarily pick up our third with your buddy, the vampire."

Rod paused, turned halfway around, and smiled at Sam.

"I didn't see him downstairs. Did you?"

"No. Maybe the maniac got him, too."

Downstairs, the panic continued. Shrill voices combined with sharp banging.

"You've seen plenty of blood in your time," Sam said. She nodded at the master bedroom door. "Lead the way."

Rod entered and followed Sam's flashlight beam to the bodies. Sam saw that the front door guard, Chris, was indeed dead. The top half of his mummy rags and his mask lay in a little heap next to his date's panties. The scene looked as if someone had dragged him off the young woman and hurled him against the nearest wall with such force that the plaster and lathing had collapsed. His date lay propped one of the corners, her neck twisted almost backward.

Sam knew from her lists that Chris was one of those with a negative blood type. While the wall behind his body and a bit of the floor around him was smeared with blood, it was not nearly enough considering how thoroughly his throat had been opened. A length of blood-soaked mummy rag lay by his left side.

Rod continued to stare at the bodies, betraying no emotion. "You're a surprisingly curious person. I understand you asked about all the donations to our bloodmobile in the past year."

"And linked many with unusual deaths," Sam said. "But how could I possibly suspect you two of being vampires? I mean, sunlight doesn't bother you. And you drink wine."

"Nor do we have long fangs. And we eat normal food. I love garlic on my pizza," Rod filled in. "And cast a reflection in mirrors. I heard you whisper to Mary in the cellar about that."

"Over the music and the sound effects?"

Rod shrugged. He smirked as he faced Sam full on. "Yes, our hearing and eyesight are exceptional. You couldn't resist luring us here to learn the truth. Now you've learned it. So, what do you plan to do?"

"Instead of letting you drink more blood –" Sam replied, doing her best to stop herself from shaking, "– you can eat lead." She drew her right-hand pistol in a smooth motion, aimed it directly at Rod's face and pulled the trigger. A 9mm bullet exploded from the barrel.

But Rod had moved. Five feet to Sam's right. So quickly that Sam had trouble following his motion as he exited the circular cast of her flashlight.

Sam swung the pistol after the darting figure and fired twice more. She heard him grunt as one of the bullets connected. He rushed her, swinging the sword as if to cleave her in half. Sam collapsed backward to the floor, watching the tip of the blade swing an inch from her nose. She fired twice more, hitting wall and then ceiling.

The bedroom's main door slammed shut.

Chest heaving from the terror clawing upward into her throat, Sam rolled over, then jumped up. The moment she stood, she reached across her waist and grabbed her second gun. She gulped down a fortifying breath, put a bullet into the door, then wrestled it open.

The hallway was empty as far as the central staircase. Just beyond, Clayton and Mary were kicking at one of the other bedroom doors. Mary's wand, which she had clutched as if it were a weapon since entering the mansion, lay twinkling on the carpet runner.

"That guy Tony has Dina!" Clayton shouted. "He popped out of this door, grabbed her, pulled her inside and locked it."

Sam jogged on rubbery legs toward her friends. "They're vampires all right. And they're fast and strong."

"Vampires? Oh great!" Clayton lamented in a shrill voice.

"Suck it up, Kemosabe!" Sam commanded. "Keep kicking!"

The three friends battered the door together. From the opposite side came a wail.

"He's killing Dani!" Clayton yelled.

"That's not Dani's voice," Mary said.

Clayton threw his full weight into the door, shoulder first. The wood around the lock splintered. Sam completed the destruction with the heel of her boot, lurched forward and paused just beyond the frame.

Tony knelt on the floor next to Dani's/Danny's unconscious form. His hands clawed at his throat, and he wheezed as if in the midst of a powerful anaphylactic attack. He rose to one knee and glowered at Sam. In response, she put three bullets into his chest. He did not die instantly, however. Having absorbed the barrage, he came up once again on one knee. This time Sam put two slugs into his head. He sprang back, gurgled for a few moments, then lay still.

"Yugoslavian my ass," Sam said. "I looked up the characters on his cap. Liga 1 isn't a craft beer; it's a Romanian soccer team."

Clayton had rushed to Dani and was pinching the gay transvestite's cheeks. "He's alive!" he rejoiced.

"Because you both did what I said and put those metal chokers around your necks," Sam said.

Clayton yanked at his bright red Lone Ranger neckerchief until it loosened enough for him to slip it over his head. He began to wrap it tightly around the wound in Dani's/Danny's wrist. "That's the very last time I do something you ask without you explaining why. Remind me to slap you silly tomorrow, girl."

Sam returned to the corridor and shone her flashlight along its carpeted length.

Clayton called after her "He was gasping because he had drunk some of her A positive blood?"

"Exactly. I had the wrong blood information put on Dani's tag. There are only seven real people here with negative types," Sam explained. "I wanted to inflate the number to make sure these two hung around the party."

Mary stared at the dead man in the Dracula costume. "He went into toxic shock because vampires can only drink negative blood."

"True for at least these two."

"So, how do we get the other one?" Clayton asked.

Sam's eyes went wide and rolled, indicating her uncertainty. "I never thought they'd attack here. There are dozens of us. We overpower him. Then we bust open the front doors, go outside and make a call to 911."

"Where is he?" Mary asked, entering the hall.

Sam nodded down the long corridor. "He must be in one of those two bedrooms on the right. Unfortunately, they have a connecting door."

"I have a screwdriver on my army knife!" someone shouted from below in the foyer. "Get out of my way!"

Sam sniffed the air. "They better get those doors open soon. That bastard Rod has set a fire." She dug into an ammo pouch on her belt and extracted a magazine clip, which she exchanged in the pistol she had emptied.

Clayton emerged into the corridor with his guns drawn. "I got Dani's bleeding stopped. Now what?"

Sam said, "Now we flank the other one from both sides." She handed her second pistol to Mary. "You and Clayton rush into the nearer bedroom, and I'll take the farther one. The instant you see him, shoot."

Sam gave a hard stare at her fellow hunters, who were obviously not as dauntless.

"Yeah, okay," Clayton said, finally.

As the three walked cautiously forward, lambent light issued from under the master bedroom door. A few moments later, smoke began to waft out.

"How's he expect to survive?" Mary asked.

"If he's as powerful as he is fast," Sam replied, "He'll rip open the attic door and jump to the ground from the roof."

They came alongside the attic access and found it still locked.

Silently, Sam signaled for Clayton and Mary to position themselves at the first bedroom entrance while she moved to the second. Once in place, she waggled her flashlight once, twice, three times.

Simultaneously, the hunters burst through their respective doors. Sam immediately retreated into the hallway and was glad she did. Rod's shape rushed out from behind the door, sword raised. She fired as he flashed by.

"Rod Cooper, type O positive my ass!" Sam shouted into the bedroom as she swung her flashlight beam back and forth. "There ain't many creatures as negative as you."

"I'll have the last laugh, bitch!" the vampire replied, his voice sounding slightly pained.

"I got you with one of my bullets," Sam declared.

"So what? We heal completely within hours," Rod returned from a black corner of the room. "I'm already on the mend."

"So, most parts of the vampire legend are wrong," Sam spoke loudly, hoping that her words would cover the advance of her partners.

"True. Like finding an entire new world but no Eldorado or Fountain of Youth."

"You were planning to burn us all right from the start."

"True again. Drink our fill here and carry several more bags of blood away in one of those ice coolers downstairs. Massive tragedy. Stupid college kids locked themselves inside a trespassed mansion and then couldn't get out as the place burned to the ground. What happened to Tony?"

"He gave a hickey to a guy who just wasn't his type. So, a bullet wound won't kill you, but a shot to the head will."

"Come in here and find out," Rod invited.

"Okay."

Sam rushed forward with her pistol extended and squeezed off a rapid succession of shots, using the bursts from the pistol muzzle and her flashlight to locate the vampire. He jinked and darted toward her with unbelievable speed. Then, suddenly, he jittered.

A barrage of bullets from the open connecting doorway to his left caught him in several places. Mary and Clayton had burst through the space with their guns blasting.

Rod aimed his cutlass at Sam as he continued forward, but she spun against the hallway wall, out of his reach. He exited the bedroom like a drunk in a sped-up movie, careening down the corridor and past the top of the staircase. As he did, Sam emptied her pistol in his direction. Clayton likewise emptied both his revolvers. Screaming with pain, Rod disappeared into the bedroom that held his former partner's corpse.

"Dani's still in there!" Clayton yelled.

The three hunters raced to the bedroom door. Sam and Mary trained their flashlights on the man in the blood-covered pirate costume. He lay face up, writhing in agony. Three of the bullet holes in his body spewed plumes of what looked like steam.

"What did you shoot me with?" Rod asked with his penultimate dying breath.

Clayton looked at the guns in his hands. "The Lone Ranger always used silver bullets. No matter the cost, I had to be completely authentic."

"Congratulations, Kemosabe," Sam said. "You lucked out on one part of the legend that's actually true. Now let's see how good you are at putting out a fire."

The Nice Man Cometh

Franklin Harrison walked wearily along the sidewalk, vacuum cleaner in one hand and demonstration case in the other, wishing he had not left his car at the top of Jonathan Drive. He had already assailed without success the first five houses on the north side of the street. Except for their exterior paint colors, every dwelling on the winding street was identical. Split-level, one-car garage, one-and-a-half baths, playroom on the ground level, open living/dining/kitchen area on the second level, three bedrooms on the third.

The year was 1952, and the collective post-war ambition was to move into the new suburban neighborhoods being thrown up at insane speeds. They and their fifth-acre yards provided much more than did pre-war, Depression apartments or duplexes in the cities, even if they were built by inexperienced laborers from inferior materials. The sheer number of such spanking new communities around Trenton, NJ, was the reason Franklin had taken the job selling Kirby vacuum cleaners. He refused to use the worst of the high-pressure techniques he had been inculcated with, trading instead on his helpful "nice man" personality rather than, for example, the tactics used by the sleazeball who had sold him his Ford.

Franklin would have made the Army his perpetual home except that they refused to reenlist him for his would-be fourth tour of duty. He had failed test after test for advancement. Having given the best years of his life to the war effort, including dropping out of high school in his senior year, he was not well prepared for civilian life. But he was convinced that a good work ethic and extra hours pounding brand new sidewalks would make him a success.

The house at the bottom of the decline was painted milk of magnesia pink. He paused to blink at it for only a moment, then slogged up to the front door, set down his demo case, and pressed on the electric bell. He heard no sound from inside. He tried again, with identical results. He looked down at the sisal mat. Instead of the almost-invariable "Welcome," the black lettering spelled out "Hals und Bein Bruch."

"Strange names," he muttered to himself. As he raised his hand to knock on the door, it opened.

Standing just inside was a woman wearing a wide smile. Franklin labored not to show his surprise. The lady of the house looked for all the world like Donna Reed in her eponymous television show. He judged her to be in her early thirties. Not a single strand of her bouffant hairdo was out of place. She wore makeup and a string of pearls around her neck. Her fingernails were polished to a fare-thee-well. Beneath her perfectly clean apron was a stylish flower-print dress. Most amazingly, she wore stockings and two-inch heels.

"Good afternoon!" Franklin chirped. "Is it Mrs. Bruch?"

"No," the woman answered, continuing to smile. "Oh! You're selling vacuum cleaners!"

"Yes, I am," he replied with an upglide, happy to receive the first truly positive greeting that day. "Might you have need of one?"

"Perhaps. Come right in!"

The woman stepped back and swept her hand invitingly inward. Her face turned as well, and her heavily lacquered hair followed a full second later.

"Why, thank you. I'm hoping to make you a happier housewife for many years to come."

"With that?" the housewife asked.

"Absolutely. Y'know, in the next thirty years you might need to buy three vacuums from the likes of Sears. But the Kirby has a lifetime guarantee."

When the woman closed the door, Franklin realized that, although the autumn afternoon sun outside was brilliant, the picture window curtains were closely drawn and that the room was lit by an overhead fixture and two free-standing lamps.

You don't say," the woman responded.

"I do say!" Franklin countered, and added a laugh. "Might I have your name?"

"Is your name Betty?"

"No."

"Then you don't have my name," she answered. Her look was so benign that he wondered if she could possibly have a mind that literal.

"Actually, I'm Frank Harrison. Well, Betty, this beautiful machine and its attachments will do half your housework."

"Half? Then you'd better sell me two."

Franklin studied the placid face staring at him, decided that Betty had a very dry sense of humor, guffawed, and said, "Good one! Now, your time is valuable, so I want to give you something practical in exchange for it."

Betty nodded at the appliance. "That vacuum."

"Well, no. But I will vacuum any space in your house to show you its amazing cleaning power."

"Sounds fair," Betty said. "How about the carpet in the upstairs hallway?"

"Wonderful." Franklin had already set down the canister-style vacuum on the playroom floor. He unsnapped his case and removed two lengths of shining pipe. As he twisted one into the other, he said, "Other companies will sell you tin that's coated by a thin layer of chrome. But we manufacture our solid hose elements from steel. Imagine –"

Before Franklin could utter another syllable, a door at the end of the room flew open and a man rushed out. Both his hands clutched large kitchen knives. His face was the embodiment of rage, flushed bright red. His eyes were huge as they settled on the lady of the house.

"Not one more moment!" he screamed. "You either open that door, or else –" He rushed toward her brandishing the knives in a lethal manner.

Franklin swung his steel pipe combination as hard as he could, striking the enraged man in the temple. The knives tumbled from his grasp. His eyes rolled into his head. He collapsed backward like a falling tree. The rear of his skull smacked hard against the playroom linoleum.

"Holy crap!" Franklin yelled. "Who is he?"

"He wants me to buy a set of knives," Betty replied, with no trace of terror at all in her voice. "Guaranteed to stay sharp forever."

"I didn't want to hurt him, but he was going to —"

"I saw. Thank you very much. You are my knight with shining attachments."

Franklin realized he had seen no other door-to-door salesman as he worked his way down the street. He wondered how he could have missed spotting the knife set peddler. "You're welcome. But why was he so angry?"

"Who knows what's in peoples' minds," said Betty. "I'm beginning to think I shouldn't let salespeople inside my house."

The felled man had not moved. Franklin knelt by his side. "I can see why. Oh, Lord! I think he's stopped breathing."

"Well, you gave him a terrible whack." Betty lifted her right hand and waggled her forefinger. "I'd better call the police."

"My Lord!" Franklin gasped.

"You spoke of time being valuable. That is so true. So, I don't want you wasting your time waiting for the police to arrive," Betty went on. "Why don't you go upstairs and vacuum the hallway outside the bedrooms right away?"

Franklin glanced at the man lying in front of him. "Really?"

"Really."

Franklin felt his legs fail him as he labored to rise.

"Well, get up!" Betty said rather sharply. "Time's a-wasting. I'll look after him as soon as I finish my call." She pointed up the six steps that led to the second level.

Franklin snatched up the vacuum cleaner and added the rug-cleaning brush attachment to the slightly bent pipe combination in his other hand. As he headed up the stairs, the Donna Reed look-alike dialed the Princess telephone on an end table next to the couch.

The vacuum cleaner pusher paused as he reached the connecting space between the living and dining rooms. As with the playroom, the drapes had been securely drawn just beyond the television set. The window that lit the dining room was of the clerestory variety, set too high to look out of. Again, artificial lighting blazed.

While Franklin pondered the scene, a man in a white uniform and cap emerged through an arch in the back side of the kitchen. In his right hand, he held a large wire basket that held a plastic-wrapped loaf of white bread, two one-pound packages of butter and three filled quart milk bottles. He opened the refrigerator, peered into it for a moment, shook his head, and turned toward Franklin.

"I've got to get out of here. Excuse me."

Franklin stepped back and allowed the milkman to pass. Curious about what he had just witnessed, he set down his demonstration equipment, walked into the kitchen, and opened the refrigerator. It was fairly filled with unopened quarts of milk, packages of butter and loaves of bread. Aside from bottles of ketchup, mustard and mayonnaise, the appliance contained nothing else. Franklin shook his head and peered through the arch from whence the milkman had emerged. Beyond it, a hallway ran far deeper than he imagined possible of the house dimensions. He thought about returning to the playroom to find out whether or not he had killed the knife set salesman but decided against it.

"Just go about your business," he told himself out loud. "You saved the woman. The police will be here at any minute, and you can't lose your opportunity to make the sale."

Franklin carried his equipment up the second set of six steps to the hall that he assumed was the one the housewife wanted cleaned. The single hallway wall outlet was blocked with an electric clock cord and a second cord that fed a wall sconce. All five doors that interrupted the hallway walls were closed. He shrugged and tried the door nearest him.

Beyond lay a bedroom that clearly belonged to a teenage girl. To Franklin's surprise, the room's owner relaxed on her bed, surrounded by stuffed animals and pillows. She wore saddle shoes, bobby sox, a poodle skirt, a wide belt and a tight, pink cashmere sweater than hugged her upper curves. A silken neckerchief covered most of her neck and her hair was held back by a pink plastic tiara. Her eyes were closed, but she seemed to be listening to a good-looking man in his late twenties who sat on the wooden chair that matched a high-gloss white desk with gold filigrees. The man, whose focus was riveted on a thick book, read to the teenager, in a tired-sounding baritone voice.

"'...a name applied to certain sea cucumbers,'" he said, "'sausage-shaped marine animals of the class Echinodermata.'" He halted and looked at Franklin as if he had only that instant registered the vacuum cleaner seller's presence.

The thought that entered Franklin's head was that there was something slightly scandalous about a handsome young man alone in a pretty teenage girl's room with her stretched out on the bed.

Franklin said, "I'm here to –"

"Sell something," the young man interrupted. "Just like me." He gestured to the wide case at his feet.

Franklin ventured forward and looked down. He saw a row of *Encyclopedia Britannica* volumes, six marked "A-Anstey" and one each of the next two volumes in the set.

"I'm Larry," the young man said, closing his book and dropping it into the case. His breathing quickened. "Did you just get here?"

Franklin looked behind him. "Well, a few minutes ago –"

"We need to get out of this place!" Larry said with clear urgency in his tired voice. "I mean, don't even try to bring whatever you're selling with you."

"Why?" Franklin asked.

"Tell him why, Tiffany," Larry said, turning toward the girl on the bed. "Tiffany! Tell him why!!"

The teenager did not react in any way to the encyclopedia salesman's shouts.

"Is she dead?" Franklin worried.

"No. Look at her chest. She's breathing. It's like she has narcolepsy."

"What?"

"A sleep disorder."

"How long has she been like that?"

"Since a few minutes after I met her. Her mother –"

"Betty."

"No. Nora. Nora asked me to read to her to see if Tiffany thought she was old enough to replace her *World Books* with the *Britannica*. I thought it was strange for her to leave me alone with this gorgeous kid, but I need the sale."

"And how long have you been reading?"

Larry shook his head ruefully. "I'm halfway through Volume 3."

"I'm Franklin, by the way. Why haven't you left before this?"

"I've tried. Come with me!"

Larry moved past the bed.

"Wait! This is the door for the hallway," Franklin said, pointing behind him. "That must be a closet."

"Come with me!" Larry repeated.

Franklin followed. Larry opened the door and stepped back to allow Franklin to see beyond.

A hallway indistinguishable from the one Franklin had just exited lay beyond. He stared at the wall clock and lighting fixture, then at the four doors farther down the space. Without a word, he reversed his movement and went to the room's other door. The same hallway lay beyond, identical except for his equipment.

"What the hell?" Franklin snapped.

"I hope you're smarter than me," Larry said. "I can't find a way out of this house! Come on!"

The two moved through the door that lay past the bed and into the hallway.

"Shouldn't this be an outside wall?" Franklin asked.

"I certainly think it should," Larry agreed. He threw open the first door they encountered. A foul smell assailed their noses.

"Good grief, what's that stink?" Franklin asked.

"It's coming from behind that door. I haven't had the courage to open it."

Franklin strode forward and grabbed the knob. "I do." He yanked the door backward.

The space beyond was a closet. Its shelves and clothing rod were empty. A man's body lay half propped up. He appeared to have been dead for about a week. On his lap was a product case. The printing on the side read: Fuller Brush.

"Jesus!" Franklin screamed. He did not linger to speak with Larry but rushed past him out of the room. He came to six steps leading down to a dining area, hurtled past it into the living room, and tore back the drapes. On the other side of the windows lay an identical living room, reversed as if the reflection of a mirror.

Franklin sprinted through the kitchen and its rear archway. He realized he had entered an identical kitchen. He ran on and encountered a set of six steps leading down to what looked like the playroom and front door. Betty or Nora or whoever had answered the door had disappeared, as had the man selling knives.

Franklin ripped at the playroom curtains, bringing them down along with their supporting rod. On the other side of the glass was the same living room he had seen twice before.

Gasping for breath, Franklin advanced on the front door. He opened it slowly. And found himself in Tiffany's bedroom.

* * *

Autumn leaves from spring-planted saplings tumbled along Jonathan Drive. Sally Monroe rang the bell of the home that lay directly across from its milk of magnesia twin. She bent and retrieved the three circular tins she had set down. The door opened, and a tired-looking young matron bouncing a cranky baby appeared, curiosity knitting her brow.

"Hi!" the visitor exclaimed. "I'm Sally Monroe."

Understanding relaxed the matron's expression. "Well, hello! Claire Di Donato. You just moved in two houses down."

"Yesterday. The paint still smells on the walls," Sally said. She offered Claire one of the three tins. "It says 'Hershey's' on the side, but it's actually filled with chocolate chip cookies I just baked. Second batch in my new oven."

Claire cleared her throat. "I think the tradition is that the old neighbors bring the treats to the new ones."

Sally smiled. "I know. But no one on this street can really be called an 'old neighbor.' And I just couldn't wait to meet everyone on the block."

"How sweet," Claire replied. She peeked past her visitor's shoulder, at the pink house. "But a word to the wise: Don't go knocking on the door of the place across the street."

The Music of the Spheres

"I have something to share with you, Ty," Louis "Majah Kee" Saunders said in his raspy, failing voice. "Before we go out on that balcony."

"What's that, Lou?" Tyrone Akachi asked. The second-most successful rap, hip-hop and gangsta recording producer in the country had pulled a straight-backed chair up close to Saunders to be able to hear him.

Composer/lyricist and producer sat in a private dressing room of Washington, DC's Kennedy Center, waiting for Saunders' public acknowledgement of their lifetime achievement award.

"First," Saunders said, "I want to apologize for all the trouble I caused refusing to have a medley of my hits performed tonight."

Akachi lifted his hands as if in defeat. "Hey, man, it's your party. I know you spent a lot of secret time on your serious music over the years, so it must be important to you. But there's gonna be a lot of confused people in the audience and in front of their TVs when that orchestra starts playing."

"More than confusion," the wheel-chair-bound man said. "You deserve to know more about my serious music. And, frankly, I've wanted to share the story for…well, thirty-one years."

Akachi glanced at the clock on the dressing room wall and saw that there was time enough to recite the entire Declaration of Independence. "All I know, all I ever wanted to know, was that it was your secret and didn't get in the way of all the music you put out for our public."

"Music?" Majah Kee, acknowledged over the years by all but Kanye West to be the king of the rap and hip-hop, rattled out a laugh. "Other than the facts that it has rhyme and rhythm, it's crap. I've been shitting out both ends for the past half century: The asshole end to stay alive, the brain end to live high and wide."

"That never would have happened if you'd stuck to serious music," Akachi said, hurt by his major star dissing what had made the both of them millions.

"Not necessarily true, my friend. Bernstein, Williams, Korngold all made fortunes."

"Who's Korngold?"

Saunders waved away the question. "German opera to Hollywood swashbucklers. What I want you to know is that I was argued into not making my serious music public."

"By who?"

"By an angel."

Now it was Akachi's turn to laugh. "Say what?"

"An honest to God angel, Ty."

"Like with wings and a halo."

"No. Angels couldn't do their tasks on Earth if they had wings and halos. This one was playing a twelve-string guitar in the subway under Lincoln Center. Not just strumming chords. Playing like Segovia."

"Who?"

"World's greatest classical guitarist. Just listen. I was a graduate-level composition student at

Juilliard at the time. Poor, but with enough spare coins to let the angel know I appreciated his skill. He was playing 'La Campanella'." Saunders looked at his producer's knotted brow. "Lizst. Paganini. Never mind. Incredibly difficult on the guitar. Not one mistake. When he had finished, I applauded. He stood and invited me to coffee. I begged off, saying I had a composition session. He was still there when I returned to the subway. This time he was playing an extremely difficult Bach fugue. Perfectly. He asked again to share coffee with him."

"An angel playing a guitar in the New York subway," Tyrone doubted.

"The King of Kings was born in a stable," Louis countered. "He got right to the point. He asked if I thought humans were the only self-aware creatures in the universe. I said that, given the billions of stars and trillions of planets, that such a situation was unlikely. Then he asked if I thought humans might be unique in any way. I supposed by our shape."

"Yeah," Akachi agreed. "Especially our ears. Ugly things."

"He said that many creatures were bilaterally organized, used two legs with feet to move, had torsos for major organs, arms and hands for using tools, necks, heads with the major sense organs up high. So, then I offered a bit of homegrown philosophy: Love is mankind's contribution to eternity. He smiled at my words and declared me an optimist. 'Love is what created the universe,' he said. 'Your kind is far more unique in terms of hatred and greed.'"

"I'm getting lost here," Ty admitted.

"This guitar-playing creature then said, 'Humans are unique. Unique by your ability to create music.' It was at this point that I asked why he separated himself from this reply. It was at this point that he declared himself to be an angel.

"'While God is a force far beyond human understanding,' he said, 'unlike your expectations, He cannot pay attention to all aspects of the universe at one time. Therefore, he sends out legions of angels in various forms, to deliver messages, to keep watch, to facilitate occasional miracles.'"

"'And what have you been sent to do?' I asked, thinking to humor a mentally unbalanced, but musically gifted individual. He answered that speaking to me was not a commandment from the Almighty but rather an outreach based on the earth-bound angels' love of our kind."

"Real nut job, huh?" Tyrone said.

Louis pursed his lips and dipped his head to one side. "You be the judge. According to this character, who revealed his angelic name to be Cherubiel, humans are the only creatures in the universe who create music beyond the mating and territorial sounds built into their genetic codes. Every song the heavenly host sing or play come from this planet."

The Rap producer relaxed back against the chair. "Well, good for our team. So that means that we're special, and God will make sure we stay around to create music for Him."

Tyrone shook his head ponderously, coughed, and said, "Actually, the opposite. According to

Cherubiel, the Creator believes we've almost fulfilled our purpose. Just a few more million notes of what He considers divine and then heaven has enough. He pulls out all the angels and leaves us completely on our own. Failed creations forsaken. Lost causes left by the Milky Wayside. I told him that was hard for me to believe."

"And he said…" Ty coaxed.

"He said that God built into us innate senses of right and wrong, which our free will rejected as often as it accepted. Then He gave us commandments, then prophets, then Yehoshua of Nazaret."

"Jesus."

"The same. We ignored the laws and the prophets, killed His son and, lately, have been destroying the planet with rampant overpopulation and misuse of resources. With the rest of the universe to oversee, He had tired of all of our rejections. So, after our kind create only a few more musical compositions that approach perfection, this corner of the galaxy is going to be ignored. Left for us to forget morality, skirt or pervert the laws, turn the world into a purely dog-eat-dog environment accompanied by the most simple-minded, banal so-called music ever set to synthesizer and autotune."

Akachi sat in silence for several seconds. "At which point you should have thanked him for the cup of coffee, fled for the door and never looked back."

"Absolutely correct," the award recipient replied. "Except that he told me much more. Things about Mozart and Gabrieli and Rimsky-

Korsakov and George Gershwin that one would only learn by knowing them personally."

"Sure. All invented from his fevered mind."

"Not like who they had bedded or what they wore stuff. What their inspirations and who their influences were. The inner workings of their compositions. How they had acquired their skills. What music they destroyed. All the way back to King David. But I was mostly swayed by how perfectly he had played that guitar."

"And you never told me any of this until now for what reason?"

"Exactly because it's incredible. Not so incredible, however, that more than a dozen of the world's best composers have also held back their works – masses, requiems, symphonies, operas – because of what Cherubiel or one of his counterparts told them."

"How do you know that?"

"Because I made it my business to find out why men and women who began their musical lives with such promise suddenly stopped serious composing. Why no new great songs and hymns and operas are being written – only bubblegum, rap, beat boxing, crunk and emo flourish. "

"The talented writers all were contacted by this Cherubiel."

"The angels all used the name 'Cherubiel', but they each looked different. Angels in female shapes approached the women; men the men. One played the piano, another the violin, a third the flute."

Tyrone scratched his beard. "So, these very gifted young composers all stopped writing serious music, just like you."

"Not only that. They all dumbed down their talents to churn out second-rate stuff. Or fourth rate, as I have." Louis' eyes rolled heavenward, and self-loathing filled his face. He intoned, "When I love dat bitch/Til I make her booty twitch/She want me and her to hitch/Which is such a friggin' stitch.' How can they honor a man who wrote and set that to a three-note melody with a I-IV-V-I chord progression repeating over and over and over and over again?"

"You wrote better stuff than that," the producer protested.

"Which is like saying I turned out Westminster Kennel Club turds as opposed to alley mongrel turds. Tyrone, I won the American Prize for Composition, the Chatauqua Institute Award and the Young American Composers blue ribbon – all before I was twenty. My works had been played by the Boston, St. Louis and Montreal Symphonies, and the New York Philharmonic."

"A couple people told me about those, but I figured it had to be another Louis Saunders."

"No. That was me. Pre-Cherubiel me."

"Damn. And you stopped because of some madman who played great guitar?"

"Heavenly guitar. That's right."

"More than thirty years ago."

"Yes. But now I'm dying, and I want my rightful due." Louis Saunders pulled himself more upright in his wheelchair. "This 'Elegy for Strings' is my finest work. Better than Britten's 'Cantus in Memoriam' or Barber's 'Adagio for Strings'. More than twenty million people will hear it tonight –

and that will rescue me from the onus of 'Majah Kee.' Sorry, Ty. No disrespect meant."

The music producer stood and began to rub the nape of his neck. "How can I take offense at something I don't even begin to understand? Well, let the show go on, because nothing like what that crazy guitar player predicted is gonna happen."

T Riffik, the latest Rap artist to hit it big, had been given the honor of introducing Louis "Majah Kee" Saunders. Squinting from mild myopia, he read the fulsome introduction off the cue cards in a near-monotone voice. When finished, the audience in the orchestra seating turned and offered Louis polite, but bridled, approbation with their applause. Then the main curtain opened, revealing a twenty-six-piece string orchestra.

 T Riffik began backing stage left. "At his personal request, our honoree offers for us the premiere of his composition, 'Elegy for Strings'."

From almost the first swish of the conductor's baton, it became obvious that the full potential of human musical creativity was on display. The camera focusing on the audience captured faces slack jawed in utter surprise, which elided into wide-eyed wonder and, from more than a few, a subtle forward movement in their seats to draw closer to the sounds that spoke the universal language directly to their emotions.

The composition lasted four minutes and fifteen seconds. When the conductor's baton dropped for the last time and the final reverberations echoed and then died, a profound silence reigned. It was the silence that signals one's presence before a thing of absolute beauty that defies description. And then, as if a prompting sign had been turned on, the entire audience erupted as one. A moment later, they stood. The adulation rolled toward the stage and up to the composer in thunderous waves.

Louis Saunders smiled and blew a kiss at the orchestra. Then, in mid-gesture, like a railroad crossing gate suspended in mid-air, his arm froze. His sweeping focus on the audience had fixed on one figure.

"He hasn't aged a day!" Saunders gasped.

"Who?" Akachi asked from his side.

"Cherubiel."

The next moment, the figure standing in the middle of the orchestral seating seemed to sprout wings. Six in all, so gossamer that Louis could see the audience just behind them. The figure smiled up at Louis and nodded, an infinitely sad expression. He bent his knees slightly and sprang straight upward, wings beating hard on the down stroke. He reached the ceiling, passed through it without slowing, and disappeared.

Collectively, the audience gasped. They looked at each other for confirmation of what they had witnessed. Then, in an age filled with sense-repudiating magical images, they all decided that this was simply a visual fillip added to the award segment. Their applause redoubled.

"I couldn't help it, Ty," Louis cried out. "I couldn't hide my real music any longer."

"That's all right," his producer friend replied. "Nobody's gonna miss things they don't believe in anyway."

The Deadliest Species

Ellison awoke from a dream of a glacial tarn. It was bounded by a horseshoe of jagged mountain peaks, surrounded by stands of birch and flowering summer weeds, and populated by buzzing insects and twittering birds. He had knelt at the edge of the lake to take in his reflection in the mirror-like water and realized that the face was not his but that of an older man.

He pushed the memory from his consciousness and concentrated on the view directly in front of him. Pure human creation. Metals and plastics and glass of various formulations. A ship. A spaceship. The Interstellar Ark. On its way to Proxima Centauri to terra-form its planet, P Centauri b. Transporting the first human colony to a planet only slightly larger than Earth and within the habitable zone. Possibly for the survival of the human species.

Ellison had been assured that the sixty-four members of the colony were the most genetically sound among those who eagerly volunteered to escape Earth. The surface of man's home had become steadily more uninhabitable from disastrous human stewardship, the refusal of human's to limit the exponential growth of his numbers, global warming, the explosion of the Yellowstone supervolcano, and a cluster of huge meteors that were not gracious enough to land in places like the most remote Russian tundra or Antarctica.

Ellison's hibernation pod tilted to ease his transfer to his exercise table. He realized that he could not remember having trained for the series of mechanically assisted maneuvers his atrophic body needed to bring it back to normal functionality. He allowed the machinery and the gentle prompting voice to guide him. To the right of his pod, his personal robo-servant waited on rubber treads to attend to all his needs until he was fully self-supporting. He tried to speak but found that his vocal bands could only make a weak, croaking sound.

I hope this is the worst of the trip Ellison thought.

To his left, another pod came to life, unsealing, humming, trading fluids.

Ursula, Ellison thought.

The initial wake-up crew numbered six. All were experts focused on the functions of the Interstellar Ark. The botanists, agriculturalists, terra-formers, miners, physicians, colony fabricators and mechanics slept on, not intended to awaken until the journey was at an end. The full complement of shipkeepers sat as one around the circular refectory table for only the third time since their awakenings. They had made nothing but small talk during food preparation, until Ellison set down his cup and cleared his throat loudly.

"Something go down the wrong pipe?" Ursula inquired.

"No. More like a thought jumped across the wrong synapse," Ellison said. "I've been wondering why the ship woke us up earlier than it should have."

Clarke, chief of medicine, and Octavia, chief of propulsion, continued to shovel food into their mouths, clearly not interested in sharing an opinion.

Isaac, in charge of all things mechanical, shook his head. "None of us had any part in the programming of our wake-up. That team evidently added a subroutine that balanced the breaking of our hibernation against the loss of that antenna array. Do you agree, Tanith?"

The head of computer engineering and informatics shrugged. "If I knew how long ago the antennae were damaged, I might be more inclined to agree with you. But what's done is done. I'm not wasting time looking for the answer in manuals or code." Tanith regarded Ellison, who served as captain and navigator. "So, when do we go EVA and fix the cluster?"

Ellison said, "What's the rush? We have so much to do inside, even given that we don't enter Proxima Centauri's system for another twenty-two cycles. The people on Earth have waited thirty years for signals from us. It's not like another thirty cycles is going to make a difference."

"Certainly not to us," Octavia added.

"What has me more concerned," Isaac said, "is that I can't convince the system to open the general hibernation chambers."

"Why do you need to enter them?" Clarke asked. "I can read the individual statuses of all fifty-eight sleepers from the helm or the Conditions console."

Isaac shrugged. "Because one up-close glance is worth a thousand lines of code. Like my great-grandfather used to say: 'You want to pop the hood and check what's in the engine compartment directly; by the time the idiot lights come on, it's too late.'"

Ellison took a sip from his cup. "As long as we have this extra time, I'll tell you what I think should be our top priority: a force shield." The faces around him took on similar doubtful expressions. Ellison raised a forefinger. "The Russian-led consortium had nearly made the breakthrough, and we have all their data. With thirty years of time to dream, I think I managed to brainstorm the missing elements. You're all aware of the toll that hundreds of mini-meteorites have taken on this ship."

"More than aware," Ursula said. "Fixing what the auto-repair system didn't take care of occupied our first two cycles."

"Both the reception and broadcast features of the antenna array can stay down a bit longer. What's that, weighed against the possibility of coming within the orbits of PC's captive objects after thirty years and being blown away by a fragment cloud?"

"How much time and energy to construct your field?" Octavia asked.

Ellison had already turned to the chamber's computer console and was energetically calling up diagrams. "Fourteen cycles maximum, and far fewer parts and energy drain than you'd think. Because it's not a static field like a soap bubble."

Clarke shrugged. "I'm in favor of mental exercise, to relieve the repair details and the tedious aerobics and isometrics. And you know what else we can assemble in that giant machine shop and the warehouse decks?"

The group waited with expectation.

"Mechanical avatars for at least two of us. Four would be even better. Why risk our own hides going EVA?"

Tanith said, "True. They should be our sizes and shapes. Even though we can engineer them not to need space suits, the magnetic shoes, the coated visors and all the packs designed to attach to our suits argue for it."

Ellison aimed his mouth at the chamber's main microphone. "Jules, show us the Proxima Centauri system."

"Showing," the genderless voice responded. The graphs Ellison had called up were replaced on curving monitors by the red dwarf star and the dim dot not far from it that was its only planet.

"You all know what they say about idle hands," Ellison said.

"I don't," Ursula responded.

Ellison's head reared back slightly. "Sure you do. Or did. You've just forgotten it."

"That may be," she said. "Enlighten me."

"And me," Tanith added.

"'Idle hands are the Devil's workshop,'" Ellison supplied.

"Let's just hope that Earth II isn't the real Devil's workshop," Isaac remarked, ending conversation for awkward seconds.

Forty-four cycles later, the helmskeepers sat together on the bridge of the Interstellar Ark, discussing whether they should send out their newly created avatars to replace the damaged antennae before or after they entered orbit around Earth II. The team had worked diligently on building the robots, assembling and installing and testing the force field that protected the forward half of the ship, recalculating the ellipse around the star that would burn off their one-eighth light speed with ablating aid of the force field, and taking full-spectrum electromagnetic readings of the star and the target planet during fleeting lowerings of the field.

"I believe we've retuned the fiddle as much as we should," Ellison said. "Any more tinkering at this point might bust a string."

"Does that include leaving the rest of the colony in their sleep pods?" Isaac asked. "Because they collectively comprise a hell of a lot of knowledge about this ship and this star system that we don't."

"The computers can supply all the hard facts we need," Ellison said.

"But in a moment?" Isaac shot back. "Computers may calculate at nearly the speed of light, but AI still doesn't have the associative capabilities we call intuition. Many hands make near-light-speed ships work."

"Also, the six of us can't possibly be everywhere in the ship," Ursula added, "monitoring all the readouts and extrapolating possible emergencies."

Ellison said, "Once we wake them, they're up for good. We won't have the provisions to support sixty four if the terra-forming is radically delayed."

"Once we initiate the hydroponic and scrubber/rebreather systems, we can go several years inside the ship. All of us," Ursula argued, looking straight at Ellison.

God, she is a pain in the ass Ellison thought to himself. It's almost as if she goes out of her way to contradict me at every turn. She's gorgeous to the eye, but how a guy whose grandparents came from Ethiopia ever found her cool Scandinavian personality attractive is beyond me. And yet I married her.

Ellison searched his memory for the first time he met Ursula. It was at a meeting of NASA engineers and suppliers. She had immediately impressed him as smart. She laughed at his jokes. She was unmarried, with no children. And she was beautiful. He remembered their first date, a drive down to Galveston to tour its railroad museum, followed by dinner at the BLVD restaurant. The next thing that popped into his head was their wedding. But for the life of him, he could not remember anything from their courtship. He worried that the prolonged space travel, even well protected in their cocoon cryogenic beds, had somehow damaged sections of his brain. Which meant that he would certainly have forgotten important training and experiences as well. He made a mental note of questioning Clarke on the subject. Ursula had been his closest workmate at NASA, but, for some reason after waking, he found himself gravitating more to the Cal Tech propulsion professor, Octavia.

Earth II had a single moon, which had been named Luna. Its orbit around the target colony planet was slower than that of the original Earth's moon. By chance, it was hidden from the Interstellar Ark until the spaceship was almost precisely one million kilometers away. Three of the ship's sails had been judged as too damaged by space debris and jettisoned. The other three had been hauled into the ship. The gargantuan nuclear fusion propulsion system was shut down, so that the Ark maneuvered purely by use of Vernier rockets. The navigational computers were engaged in turning the ship for a fly-by analysis of Luna when a potent beam of laser light issued from the moon, raking the skin of the Ark's bow. Only the high reflective index of the aluminum alloy saved the ship from being immediately pierced.

An instant after the first contact, the ship's force field blossomed. As it absorbed the laser energy a spectacular show began, akin to the Northern Lights where Earth I's magnetic force is weak. No alarm system had been built into the force field, since it had been designed to protect the Ark from benign natural phenomena such as meteor impacts and solar winds. Ellison had been on the ship's bridge, speaking with Isaac, his back toward to the monitors and viewing port. Isaac's surprised refocus past Ellison's shoulder and the sudden bursts of illumination coloring the bridge walls caused him to turn.

Ellison sprang to the console.

"What's happening?" Isaac said, scrambling into his seat. "What are you doing?"

"We're being attacked. I'm responding with the crater makers."

The ship carried forty missiles, each with the explosive force of one thousand tons of TNT. They were the equivalents of B54 Special Atomic Demolition Munitions, known during the period of the American/Soviet Cold War as backpack or suitcase nukes. Those were designed for limited nuclear warfare against overwhelming numbers; the versions on the Ark were intended as instruments of terra-forming, to create strategically placed crater areas on Earth II which would become eventual feeder lakes and sheltering coves or protective hills against high-velocity wind storms.

"They're dirty," Isaac reminded the captain.

"What else do we have?" Ellison replied. "And why should we care? We're not going to live on Luna."

The computers pinpointed the area of the moon's surface from which the laser beam originated. Ellison released a pair of the bombs.

Ursula came onto the bridge. "What's blasting us?"

"Focused light from Luna," Ellison reported. "Makes sense to put a sentry post there. No atmosphere to absorb the beam."

"Whose sentry post? Our readings detected no high forms of life on Earth II."

"It must be from an advanced life form," Ellison said.

"I don't understand," Ursula said. "Something's alive on Luna?"

Ellison adjusted the ship's pitch so that the bridge and the force field directly faced the continued laser onslaught. "Probably not. My best guess is a purely mechanized exploratory craft was sent from some distant star system, intended to claim and hold this system until the beings that built it arrive. How long it's been down there is anybody's guess."

"Aliens," Isaac said. "Incredible. But what else could it be? Well, possession is nine-tenths of the law. Even intergalactic law. We're here in person, with nowhere else to go. Humans trump machines."

"Which means war," Tanith said, signaling her entrance to the bridge alongside Clarke, the medical chief.

"But we're not a warship," Clarke said.

"Then we make ourselves into one," Ursula answered. "The ship's machine shop and warehouse decks were meant for building a colony, but first we'll have to use them to fabricate shields and weapons larger than the handguns in stock."

"How long can your force field repel the attack?" Octavia worried.

Ellison looked up from the telescope screen. "The field is actually absorbing the beam's energy, growing stronger. We should be out of its line of fire within an hour. Within four hours, our nukes should have landed. With any luck, they'll have destroyed whatever's down there."

The wake-up crew stared at the various monitors in silence. Then Isaac said, "Well, we can't go into planetary orbital mode until we're sure we're safe."

"No, course not," Ellison responded. "We'll trade off even more speed with another swing around PC. While we do, we heed what Tanith said: This is total war. War for our survival. War for control of this system. We formulate a strategy and a Plan B. We modify one of the shuttles into a fighting machine."

"And we should wake up at least those members of the colony who had military experience," Isaac said.

Ellison nodded. "Any breakthroughs in getting the main sleeper chambers open?"

Isaac shook his head grimly. "It's as if the ship is also our enemy. Like it doesn't trust us."

"Can we manufacture a false emergency to convince the program that the sleepers are in danger?" Clarke asked.

Isaac's eyes grew wide. "You want to do that, let it be on your head. Not me. If we crack those fifty-eight eggs, we can't go back to the grocery store for more."

The brilliant, shimmering curtain of ionized light continued to illuminate the forward monitors.

Ellison said, "Life or death, mates. Life or death."

Almost sixty Earth cycles had elapsed since the attack on the Ark. The images of Earth II and her moon loomed on the monitors. One of the gargantuan starship's three shuttle modules had been modified into a flying tank, with a new, light-but-sturdy exoskeleton of composite armor. A 120mm smoothbore cannon was added to the top of the lander, a weapon capable of blowing a hole through inches of hardened metal. Within the guts of the shuttle were four "Matrix" seats, named after the old sci-fi film. From within their confines Ellison, Isaac, Tanith and Clarke could operate the four avatars that were built to fit inside their EVA suits.

The plan to destroy the alien outpost also involved Ursula and Octavia operating offensive actions from the main ship. All elements had been completed seven full cycles before reaching the three-million-kilometer boundary to the orbits of Earth II and Luna. Practice exercises were run, assessed and run again.

Two Terran cycles before the assault on Luna was to begin, Ellison found himself in the aft part of the ship, beyond the warehouse decks, helping Octavia with adjustments to the nuclear reactors.

"How did you first meet Clarke?" Ellison asked, speaking of Octavia's mate.

Octavia did not need to pause from torqueing the hex wrench in her hands. "It was a setup by our mutual friend, Eric Buchanan."

"Love at first sight?"

"No. I wouldn't say that."

"So, when did you know you were hopelessly in love?" Ellison went on.

Now Octavia paused. "I can't say either of us ever reached that level."

"How long are you together?"

"Three years before beginning this journey."

"Well, it must have grown for you to still be together."

"I suppose."

"You're having children as soon as we establish the colony."

"Of course. We wouldn't have been chosen if we didn't want children. Why all the questions?"

"I've been reviewing my relationship with Ursula."

"Oh?"

"Do me a favor," Ellison said. "Remember for me what you did to celebrate each of your anniversaries together."

Octavia thought for several moments with her eyes open, then shut them. When she opened them again, her expression had changed to one of mild bewilderment. "You know, I can recall driving up to the wine country from the Jet Propulsion Lab and staying at a lovely inn with a spa."

"The Milliken?" Ellison asked.

"Yes. Exactly. In Napa."

"We stayed there for one of our anniversaries, too."

Octavia unsealed a nutrition bar. "Small world."

"Another time out to Hawaii. Business/pleasure trip."

"For a conference."

"In Ka'anapali."

"We stayed at the Royal Lahaina."

Ellison shook his head. "Sounds like we should have run into each other. But we didn't."

"I don't think so. It's kind of foggy. One anniversary is a complete blank."

"For me, as well." He touched Octavia's shoulder lightly. "I swear this longest trip in human history has affected my memory. It seems spotty."

"Yes," Octavia granted. She had stopped chewing and stared hard into Ellison's eyes.

"I...I have to tell you something," he said, "but I'm afraid it may cause real trouble."

"Go ahead."

"You never actually married Clarke."

"That's right."

"Perhaps because you thought you might find that deep love with someone else?"

Octavia's eyes drifted slightly. "I don't know."

"Well, I did marry Ursula. But since we've awakened, I'm increasingly convinced it was a mistake. We're the same age; we connect on an intellectual level; she's physically attractive to me. Our Circadian rhythms correspond, and the computer assures me that our pheromones are strongly compatible. But our personalities seem just too different."

Octavia nodded. "I've noticed."

"On the other hand, I find it much easier to talk with you." Ellison snapped his fingers. "Like when I said, 'I can't wait to get down to Earth II, because we'll have much more space,' and you laughed. Ursula didn't. I don't even know if she understood the pun's irony."

Octavia's laughter was an echo of the moment. "I understand. And I admit I've enjoyed working with you. I don't remember you being so interesting before the launch. But divorce isn't something you should contemplate rashly. Especially given the stress we're under right now."

"You're right," Ellison said.

"Committing to any kind of exclusive relationship is premature," Octavia added, "given that there are fifty-eight others onboard."

Ellison understood precisely. Among the sleepers were thirty-two females and only twenty-six males, all between the ages of 26 and 32. The expectation was that a few males would father children by more than one female.

Ellison said, "And yet it keeps staring me in the face, stress or not."

Octavia shrugged. "Tuck it away until we win this war we never anticipated." She pointed to the lubricant pack just behind Ellison.

"The outpost crater should be visible within the next fifteen minutes," Ursula announced from the captain's chair on the bridge of the Ark. "Is everything five by five from your side?"

Ellison's eyes roamed across the shuttle instrument banks. Then he glanced at the other members of the landing crew: Isaac, Tanith, and Clarke. "Roger. All LS 1 readings are nominal."

"Initiating drop sequence in five, four, three…" Octavia announced.

The inner bay doors opened, and Landing Shuttle 1 slid forward. As soon as the oxygen was claimed from the launch chamber, the outer doors opened.

"Radio silence from this point," Ellison said. He shut down the communications. It would only be re-opened if the shuttle attack crew were in a desperate situation or after the alien defenses were destroyed.

The plan was for the Ark to cut across Luna at an angle that exposed her force field for no more than ten minutes. In that time, the effects of the suitcase nuclear bombs would be assessed, and reconnaissance photos of the outpost crater would be taken. If the outpost had survived, this act was hoped to be enough to divert attention from the attacking shuttle until it was well beyond observation. A route had been mapped to land the craft close to the outpost crater, allowing a quick strike.

Three minutes after radio silence was established, Clarke began making inarticulate but excited noises from his station.

"What's going on, Clarke?" Ellison asked.

"I have both the visible- and infrared-gathering telescopes focused on Earth II, maximum magnification. I believe there are buildings down there!"

Isaac unbuckled from his seat. "Let me see." After a few moments, he said, "What? Those square green things?"

"Yes. They could be roofs with plant insulation on the tops."

"Or merely vegetation growing on huge blocks of stone."

"And what about the flashes of light? Looks like a large solar array to me."

"Or reflections from a lake butted up against the blocks of stone. We found no signs of any higher life forms, remember?"

Ellison broke in. "Priorities. Retrain and focus your instruments on the target crater! We can't signal the ship to use the bigger scopes right now, but we will after we've brought down this outpost."

Set-down was accomplished without incident. Minutes later, a single drone was sent out from LS 1, to assess the damage inflicted by the pair of backpack bombs. Isaac guided the mechanical scout, making sure to keep it only a couple meters above the moon's surface. The rest of the team members watched the monitors intently.

"What?" Ellison cried out with disbelief. "Where are the blast craters?"

The crater looked almost precisely as it had when the laser attack occurred. The only difference was the intense sparkling of the surface.

"Our nukes hit the area for sure," Isaac said. "They turned the silicon into glass."

Tanith added, "And look at the crater edges. Black streaks from incineration. I think whatever's in there not only deflected or absorbed the energy but also repaired the surface."

"Pan the drone," Ellison commanded.

The slow, sweeping visual revealed a collection of reception, broadcast and measuring devices and the apparent barrel of the laser cannon poking up from near the center of the kilometer-wide crater.

"How could those delicate instruments have escaped annihilation?" Clarke asked his fellow crew mates.

"Impossible," Ellison answered. "Unless they were retracted before the missiles landed."

"The outpost must be buried a good distance below the surface," Tanith said.

Isaac reversed the panoramic scan. "And it must be huge. Can you all see the four small instrument groupings poking up? I'd say seventy meters from the central array."

The four groupings lay equidistant from each other, forming a cross pattern.

"We may need to return to the Ark and bring down a half dozen of the nuke packs," Isaac said. "Lob them into the crater from here, so the outpost has no time to erect its defenses."

Ellison shook his head. "And irradiate whoever lobs them? Plus, who knows if the aliens haven't invented a force field. Waste a total of eight nukes on speculation? No. First we see if we can damage their laser cannon. Then we blind those instruments with the solar sails."

Isaac's avatar stood motionless in the shuttle's Lock Two. He had volunteered to climb the outer crater wall closest to the LS 1, sight in on the laser cannon's barrel with a rifle based on the legendary Barrett M82 but with custom 60mm shells. The objective was to take down – or at least damage – the cannon. The bigger version of the M82 prototype would have weighed 36 pounds on Earth I, but on Luna it was a fraction as heavy and no problem for the automaton.

While the computer chief moved to the storage chamber that housed the four robotic copies of members of the attack team, Ellison and Clarke connected the human Isaac to the recently designed avatar system. When the 3D goggles were placed over his eyes and the stereo buds placed in his ear canals, the command section of the shuttle disappeared for him, replaced by the sights and sounds inside Lock Two.

The lock opened. Isaac descended the ramp, stepped onto Luna's surface and immediately lurched sideways, misjudging the depth of the soft dust overlaying the crust. He used the sniper rifle as a walking stick to balance himself. He looked down through the helmet to the limit of its curve, checking that he still carried on his suit belt the single instrument that served for communications and targeting. Moving first cautiously and then with greater and greater confidence, Isaac climbed the crater impact ejecta. The airless world transmitted no sound of his progress. Because the avatar had no need to breathe, the advance was equally silent inside the space suit.

When he reached the crater rim, Isaac went into a crouch, then lowered himself flat against the surface. The instrument from his belt told him precisely how high to elevate his sights to compensate for Luna's slight gravity. He pushed the tinted helmet visor up and set the rear sight of the rifle against the helmet glass.

Isaac pulled back slowly on the weapon's trigger. He watched as, a second later, the cannon shook from a glancing blow. The rifle held ten rounds, and he squeezed them off as quickly as he could re-aim. When he set down the weapon to assess the damage, he saw no evidence of destruction. The only effect was that the central array began to sink beneath the sea of dust.

Growling with frustration inside the shuttle, Isaac commanded his avatar to retreat.

As quickly as he could, Isaac turned his avatar self over and began moving down the barren decline. The low gravity allowed him to spring up and move in long, loping hops. When he was within thirty meters of the shuttle, he faltered at the sight of a dozen drones exiting Lock Two. The front pair fired mini motion-seeking rockets.

Just as Isaac reached the front edge of the lock ramp, he became aware of the primitive touch sensor in his left arm signaling an impact. Simultaneously, his disconnected mechanical arm flew past him.

Isaac's awareness struggled to retreat back into his own head. When he did, he found one of the gimbaled monitors directly in front of his face. The screen showed a pitched battle among two squads of drones. He easily discerned those that had issued from the shuttle, because he had been the designer and builder of their alterations. The enemy seemed to have launched half as many drones, but they were bigger, faster, and armed with ping-pong-size balls that impacted targets with crippling shrapnel.

"Damn!" Tanith said from behind Isaac. "This makes me wonder if they've been monitoring Earth broadcasts. They don't look very different from ours."

"Drones are pretty simple inventions; no need to be different," Isaac commented. "What's strange is that the aliens must have planned to defend from Luna's surface before they even launched from their home. Their maneuvering jets are built for airless flight rather than repurposed as

I had to do to the propeller arms on ours. How badly was I hit?"

"Major repairs will be needed," Clarke answered.

"Can we jam their frequencies?" Isaac asked.

"Trying," Tanith replied. "So far, nothing."

In spite of the evasive capabilities of both sets of drones, six from the Ark and two of the enemy's squad drones were destroyed. The four remaining enemy drones zoomed over the crater rim and a tight formation.

Isaac said, "I don't know if I'm more angry or frightened."

"I'm more determined," Ellison replied. "Time to make a tactical retreat."

Tanith and Ellison took the shuttle helm, speaking to each other in soft but urgent voices as the craft's treads and bogies rattled and bounced over the rough meteor impact ejecta.

"Now what?" Isaac asked, ripping the last of the electrodes from his skin.

"Immediately to Step Two," Ellison answered. "We cover the shuttle with one sail and use the drones to drop the least damaged sail directly over their central set of sensors. Then we see what comes out to remove the second sail and shoot it to pieces with the M99 or the cannon above us."

The shuttle was large and heavy, designed for transporting materials and not for hit and run warfare. It had three sets of treads on each side: front, middle and rear. Until just before the vehicle landed, they had been retracted into the bottom of the hull. While the inner side of the crater appeared almost unaffected by the double nuclear bomb attack, plenty of rocks, some as large as fire hydrants, had been scattered on the outer side.

"I wish this thing would move faster," Tanith worried aloud, "Since we know nothing about our opponents, we have no idea what to expect."

Ellison steered around a field of jagged boulders. "Nor do they from us. They're obviously not wounded badly enough. I'm hoping their algorithms don't expect an immediate second attack. We're decamping a little way beyond the place we landed. First order of business is to camouflage the shuttle. We activate the remaining drones for observation duty while we do that. Then we go EVA."

"'We' personally?" Tanith asked.

"Our avatars."

"We only have three-and-a-half left," Isaac reminded.

"Which means we must use them with more caution. We stay out only long enough to spread the sail, spray it with glue, dredge it over the dust and secure it to the top of the shuttle. Then back inside. Their drones may not be sophisticated enough to find us under cover."

"And then we program the drones to carry the corners of the largest sail and drop it on their center array," said Isaac. "But while our drones are transporting the sail, they'll have impeded vision. We need to post one of us on the crater rim as forward observer. Who volunteers his or her automaton?"

"I do," said Clarke. "With a piece of dusty sail covering me."

"Their logic might well assume we returned to the mother ship," Isaac said. "But we hide in plain sight. I mean, how could they suspect they would run into something as smart as Homo sapiens in this part of the galaxy?"

"If they've been monitoring all the broadcast wavelengths from old Earth they could," Clarke said.

"If they've been watching television, so much the better," Tanith rejoined. "They'll assume we're a race of idiots and underestimate us."

"I observed a cut in the outer crater rim as we landed," Ellison reported. "Shaped like an arroyo."

"Arroyos are created by water," Clarke said. "No water here."

Ellison refused to waste time addressing the pedantry. "Then a gully, a gulch, a cut. I'll back the shuttle into it. Here it is just ahead. Isaac, take the helm. Tanith and I will go EV with our avatars. Clarke's will reconnoiter."

The Ark had been well stocked with M19 rifles, NATO 12-gauge assault shotguns and plenty of ammunition and magazines. Using only a pair of helmets from their space suit supply, Tanith and Ellison left the shuttle in their avatar identities, armed with shotguns and carrying knives to cut apart the sail.

Ellison took the lead, looking for the smoothest stretch of terrain to lay down the pre-cut pieces of silver-surfaced, delicately thin sail material. He was less than a minute into his search when Tanith tapped his shoulder. Ellison turned.

Tanith held an intertwined jumble of color-coded electrical wire. She pointed up the gully. Like Isaac's avatar had been, she and Ellison were committed to radio silence.

Ellison pointed in the direction of the rolled-up sails and then held his index finger aloft. Next, he pointed to where Tanith had indicated and held up both index and middle fingers, signaling their priorities. Tanith shook her head, but Ellison had already returned to search. Within a short time, all the sail material had been sprayed and dredged.

Before Ellison could move one rectangle of sail to cover the shuttle, Tanith grabbed his arm and tugged him farther into the gully. After only a few following steps, he saw that a metal hatch stood vertically in the shadow of the crater wall, half hidden by a pile of dust. The hatch had no markings and no handle or keyhole. They finished covering the shuttle, collected Clarke and retreated inside.

"So strange that these aliens would use electrical wire the same way we do," Ellison marveled to the shuttle team.

"Not really," Tanith countered. "As far as we know, the same laws govern the universe. Many metals conduct electricity. The core of those wires looked like copper. Copper is an efficient, fairly inexpensive conductor. And it has to be insulated to prevent leakage and shorts."

"What about the color coding?"

"As long as the makers sense the visible spectrum just as we do, that's just a predictable element." She smirked at Ellison. "What do you think? It's space junk from an Earth satellite?"

"I don't –"

"Forget the wire," Isaac broke in. "That hatch probably protects a tunnel that runs all the way to the outpost. I say we torch through it and launch an assault before they do. Good offense being the best defense."

"You aren't doing any torching," Clarke said. "Your avatar has only one arm. My turn this time."

"And me," Tanith quickly added. "I found the hatch."

"I'll protect your backs from the rim above the tunnel entrance," Ellison decided. He turned his attention to Isaac. "We need you to provide communications links if any of us get in trouble."

"Wonderful," Isaac said, his reply dripping with irony.

Ellison stood. "All right. First, we cover the shuttle; then we bring the fight to them."

The acetylene and oxygen for the shuttle blowtorch were almost exhausted by the time the hatch was cut open. Beyond, a tunnel with a flat floor and arching walls that vaulted three meters ran slightly downward and perfectly straight as far as the reach of the explorers' torch lamps. Clarke and Tanith retreated to the shuttle to confer. Composite shields were quickly created, to counter the likelihood that the tunnel would continue to run straight and offer no protection.

Again, Tanith and Clarke entered what Clarke called "the mole hole." She carried an assault shotgun and he brandished an M19. The walls of the accessway were smooth, as if created by a large boring machine. They found no signage. Machinery thrummed from the opposite end of the tunnel. Approximately 100 meters from the center of the crater, the floor became parallel with Luna's surface. Tanith advanced first.

A fusillade of bullets smashed into Tanith's shield, causing her to drop to one knee. Clarke dashed forward and sprayed the end of the tunnel with the full contents of a 100-round magazine of 7.62 ammunition. The velocity of the projectiles had almost doubled since use decades before in Iraq, Afghanistan, Venezuela and Liberia. The weapon was lighter than its predecessors, so that Clarke's avatar had no trouble resisting its kick from behind his shield.

The opposing firepower redirected to Clarke. Tanith took the opportunity to retreat up the incline.

Vicious as Clarke's firepower was, the barrage from the other end of the tunnel was even stronger. Little by little, his shield was being destroyed. Clarke backed up, but suddenly the shield crumpled and Clarke's avatar took a dozen quick impacts. He fell still.

From his post at the crest of the crater rim, Ellison spotted two enemy drones rising from the outpost's central array. They separated and flew in looping paths that would put them at opposite sides of the crater. Ellison crawled backward for a half-dozen meters, then stood and hopped into the gully. His plan was to place himself just inside the breeched tunnel hatch, where he could protect the hidden shuttle. When he entered, he was only mildly surprised to see the flashes of ricocheting bullets off the tunnel walls.

Tanith retreated behind her half-destroyed shield. Suddenly, a stray bullet caught her avatar just below the left knee. She fell awkwardly to the tunnel floor, recovered and flipped herself over, crawling back toward the hatch.

Enough of this defensive action, Ellison thought. The moment the drone attack breaks off, I'm going to aim our roof cannon into this tunnel and keep firing 120 mm shells until there's nothing left of that outpost. Knowing that there was no more need to stay silent, he activated his communications.

"Isaac, put on a suit and exit Lock One! Enemy drones on their way."

"Roger."

Ellison knew the magnitude of what he was asking. Isaac himself and not his avatar would be exposing himself. But there was no way he could take down both drones himself. He placed himself in the center of the hatch opening and raised his shotgun. He waited, counting the seconds. Evidently, the drones were making methodical surveys of the entire crater rim. More time passed. He looked anxiously for Isaac to appear.

One of the enemy drones swept by the gully. Ellison noted that it had slowed slightly just before it disappeared.

"Hurry up, Isaac!" Ellison radioed.

A drone appeared from the far side of the shuttle. Whether or not it was the same one that had passed seconds earlier was impossible for Ellison to tell. Tanith's radio voice sounded in his head.

"Clarke's avatar is down," she reported. "I can see you ahead, Ellison. Behind me, the firing has stopped, but the other end of the tunnel is filled with light and I can hear an engine approaching."

"Stop where you are and hold your position for as long as you can," Ellison directed.

"That won't be long."

The enemy drone seemed to have learned the effective reach of the shotguns. It neared Ellison in a hesitating fashion, then stopped. It fired one of its ping-pong-ball-shaped projectiles, but Ellison was ready. He swung swiftly around behind the protection of the hatch's bulkhead. The missile's shrapnel scattered, but not a bit of it hit Ellison's avatar.

"Here's some of your own medicine!" Isaac cried out from under the canopy of the solar sail. He had the muzzle of the M99 aimed at the shadow cast by the drone.

Ellison registered the fierce kick of the giant sniper rifle and saw the simultaneous disintegration of the attacking drone.

"Yes!" Isaac exulted. He walked toward Ellison.

Ellison watched with dismay as the enemy second drone appeared directly behind Isaac. He opened his mouth to call out a warning. Before he could, the drone stopped dead, then plummeted onto the camouflaged shuttle.

"The engine stopped," Tanith reported. "And the light is dimming. What happened?"

"I don't know," Ellison replied. "Maybe just a temporary reprieve. Let's get ourselves and our robots into the shuttle and blast the tunnel with our cannon. "

The remnants of Clarke's avatar lay inside the tunnel. Inside the shuttle, Clarke rested in his seat, laboring to master his mild shock.

"I think I may know what it feels like to die," he told his crewmates.

"I don't want to know," Tanith came back.

The four mates spoke in urgent bursts as Tanith and Ellison busied themselves with maneuvering the shuttle and Isaac explored the captured drone. The drone lay shackled to the refectory table. Isaac had figured out how to unload the machine's ammunition and was prying at the pressure tabs that protected the machine's innards.

"I got it," Isaac crowed. He had popped a cover, exposing the object's insides. "No. How can this be? Phillips head screws?"

"This is no time to joke," Tanith said, rising to get a better look.

"I'm not joking. Oh, merciful Creator!" Isaac exclaimed. "This sub unit has English words. And this one has German."

"Uh, folks…" Clarke said in a breathless tone. His stare was fixed on the monitor that was linked to an exterior camera. "Something's coming out of the tunnel."

All attention transferred from the drone. A robot with the shape of late-twentieth century bomb defusers had appeared. It cradled Clarke's broken avatar in its arms. It rolled forward on a pair of treads.

"That's the same tread design as the ones right under us," Isaac said.

The robot came to a stop and appeared to be waiting.

"Look at that design on the side of its neck," Ellison said. "Somebody zoom the camera in on it."

Even before the image had doubled in size, the six colonists sucked in simultaneous shock breaths.

"How…" Clarke said, unable to end his question.

"That's the Golden Record, the same one etched into the side of every object after Voyager 2 that left the solar system," said Tanith.

"Absolutely," agreed Isaac, narrowing his eyes to focus on the two hemispheres of Earth contained inside the symbol for infinity. "I think —"

"Stop! Not another word," Ellison ordered. "Let's learn the truth firsthand."

The outpost robot followed the four members of the shuttle crew in silence. It had no speakers to reassure the group, but its passive movements made clear that no more aggression would be encountered.

At the far end of the tunnel lay an open airlock. The outer walls shone in brilliant gold when the crew's torches were trained on them.

The group entered a small chamber and waited until the outer hatch closed. As soon as it did, a breathable atmosphere rushed into the space. The disappearance of vacuum resulted in more and more sounds penetrating the four space suits.

"Atmosphere nominal," a recorded human voice announced. The inner lock hatch slid back.

Within a few tentative steps, the crew saw that they were inside a spaceship whose dimensions and features were very much like that of the Interstellar Ark. Signage in English and a hybrid of Esperanto were affixed along the walls, as were diagrams that showed the ship to be perfectly circular. The largest passageway led to the center of the ship. One after the other, the crew removed their helmets and set them down alongside the rifles and shotguns they had carried in spite of Ellison's assurance that they would not be needed.

Tanith was the first to press the button that opened the seal into the bridge. A moment after she did, the chamber lighting began winking on. The space was illuminated by more than a thousand lights of all sizes, shapes and colors.

"Welcome, crew of the Interstellar Ark," Ellison's voice greeted from several speakers distributed around the chamber. Simultaneously, a near-perfect hologram of Ellison appeared in front of the main viewing monitor. This man, however, appeared to be more than a few years older than the one who stood frozen at the side of the ship's helm.

"I am Mostafa Tasifa," the image said. "My clone is Ellison. All of you are clones of persons from Earth, as are the other fifty-eight pilgrims.

Because of the limited speed of your ship, it was deemed that colonists would not endure the journey as full-grown individuals. Therefore, you hibernated as parent cells for much of your trip.

"This ship in which you stand is called the Golden Phoenix. It is a product of a set of discoveries soon after your launch that allow radical increases in our ability to cross space. The Phoenix was built only nine years after your ship but reached the Proxima Centauri system eight years ahead of your scheduled arrival.

"We immediately began modifying P Centauri b. Although the planet's stronger gravity put pressures on our Earth I bodies, we flourished. A small town was created, with the same plans that fill your computers. We made many adjustments to our lives in order to deal with the red dwarf star. What we could not have predicted, however, was the negative influences of the two massive Centauris. Mostly a combination of wavelengths produced during flares that proved lethal over time. Every member of our colony has been permanently affected. We will all be dead approximately three years before you arrive. This is why our machinery has been sending warning signals toward your ship.

"We know the temptation will be for you to try to devise methods to defeat the dangers of this system. However, we believe this is a forlorn exercise. Instead, we beseech you to continue on your quest for a new home, using this ship and its astonishing capabilities. You will note that, on the remote chance that another species challenges you for your eventual new home, we have created several defense systems, including a force field. The logs of our history, the instructions on using this ship, and the new features we built while in space are all available from the main computers."

Mostafa Tasifa smiled sadly into the camera lens. "The best of fortune to you."

The three-dimensional image vanished.

Contrary to the misgivings of the crew, the food created by the Phoenix was quite tasty. When all four members were seated at one of the refectory tables, Ellison threw out his hands.

"Okay. The ban is lifted. You now have permission to share your thoughts."

Isaac said, "The problems began when a meteor took out the communications array on the Ark. We couldn't receive the Phoenix's transmissions. Therefore, we couldn't reply to it. Our silence to their automated hailing was perceived as an alien species trying to claim this star system."

Clarke added, "And your creation of avatars prevented the Phoenix from detecting us as humans here on Luna."

'Not to mention our radio silence," Tanith added.

"Until we broke it."

"It's no wonder we all feel as if we have large gaps in our memories," Ellison said. "The Earth I technicians were no doubt limited in the time to create the images, sounds and so forth that we do have. As it is, they must have produced the equivalent of a hundred films that each of us starred in."

"I wonder if these computers will have more biographical information on our donors," Tanith said.

"What does it matter?" Isaac returned. "We're only them in terms of nature, not nurture." He nodded to himself. "They might as well be our fathers and mothers. I think we were prevented from visiting the other fifty-eight pods because the trip designers didn't want the six of us to be freaked out by seeing only partially developed bodies."

"You asked 'what does it matter' about our donors' lives?" Ellison said to Isaac. "It matters a whole lot to me if Mostafa was married to Ursula, or whatever her name was."

"I wonder where our names came from?" Clarke said.

Tanith sighed. "We'll probably never know. Just like we'll never know what it was like to live on 'the little blue marble'."

"So," Ellison said, "it's not as if we have a choice. Our birthing pods will become hibernation pods. And we will shortly be on our way to Gliese 832 c."

"With the hope that there won't be any other higher species claiming it," said Clarke.

Ellison glanced at the rifles and shotguns stacked at the refectory entrance. "That's not as big a fear as I had a few cycles ago. We may not be the only intelligent species of life in the universe, but we're probably the deadliest."

About the Author

Brent Monahan has spent his life fascinated with and passionate about questioning the world – and arriving at unique, thoughtful, insightful and, quite often, spear-tip pointedly amusing answers that find their expression in his many novels. Whether he is offering a rational explanation to an historical haunting, as in *The Bell Witch: An American Haunting*, or delving into the psyches and machinations of such icons of financial and political power as J.P. Morgan in *The Jekyl Island Club*, Mr. Monahan does so with an unparalleled depth of research and smart, witty writing that has engaged decades of readers and garnered him considerable critical recognition from both reviewers and his peers.

Mr. Monahan has authored sixteen novels, two of which have been made into movies – including *An American Haunting*, starring Donald Sutherland and Sissy Spacek. He has taught writing at Rutgers University and Westminster Choir College of Rider University, even though his terminal degree was in musical arts from Indiana University, Bloomington. He lives in Yardley, Pennsylvania.

www.ingramcontent.com/pod-product-compliance
Lightning Source LLC
Chambersburg PA
CBHW030134180626
46812CB00002B/693